Peak P

Samantha Alexander lives in Lincolnshire with a variety of animals including her thoroughbred horse, Bunny, and a pet goose called Bertie. Her schedule is almost as busy and exciting as her plots – she writes a number of columns for newspapers and magazines, is a teenage agony aunt for BBC Radio Leeds and in her spare time she regularly competes in dressage and showjumping.

RIDERS

3

Peak Performance

SAMANTHA ALEXANDER

MACMILLAN CHILDREN'S BOOKS

First published in 1997 by
Macmillan Children's Books
a division of Macmillan Publishers Ltd
25 Eccleston Place, London SW1W 9NF
Basingstoke and Oxford
www.macmillan.co.uk

Associated companies throughout the world

ISBN 0 330 34535 4

Copyright © Samantha Alexander 1997

The right of Samantha Alexander to be identified as the
author of this book has been asserted by her in accordance
with the Copyright, Designs and Patents Act 1988.

All rights reserved. No reproduction, copy or transmission
of this publication may be made without written permission.
No paragraph of this pub publication may be reproduced, copied or
transmitted save with written permission or in accordance with
the provisions of the Copyright Act 1956 (as amended). Any
person who does any unauthorized act in relation to
this publication may be liable to criminal prosecution
and civil claims for damages.

5 7 9 8 6 4

A CIP catalogue record for this book is available from the British Library.

Phototypeset by Intype London Ltd
Printed by Mackays of Chatham plc, Chatham, Kent

This book is sold subject to the condition that it shall not,
by way of trade or otherwise, be lent, re-sold, hired out,
or otherwise circulated without the publisher's prior consent
in any form of binding or cover other than that in
which it is published and without a similar condition including
this condition being imposed on the subsequent purchaser.

For Telephoon. With love.

Samantha Alexander and Macmillan Children's Books would like to thank *Horse and Pony* magazine for helping us by running a competition to find our cover girl, Sally Johnson. Look out for more about the **Riders** and **Hollywell Stables** series in *Horse and Pony* magazine and find out more about Samantha by reading her agony column in every issue.

Macmillan Children's Books would also like to thank Chris White; and David Burrows and all at Sandridgebury Stables, especially Toby and his owner Sylvie.

And finally thanks to Angela Clarke from Ride-Away in Sutton-on-Forest, Yorkshire for providing the riding clothes, hats and boots featured on the covers.

CHARACTERS

Alexandra Johnson   Our heroine. 14 years old. Blonde, brown eyes. Ambitious, strong-willed and determined to become a top eventer. Owns Barney, a 14.2 hh dun with black points.

Ash Burgess   Our hero. 19 years old. Blond hair, blue eyes, flashy smile. Very promising young eventer. He runs the livery stables for his parents. His star horse is Donavon, a 16.2 hh chestnut.

Zoe Jackson   Alex's best friend. 14 years old. Sandy hair, freckles. Owns Lace, a 14.1 hh grey.

Camilla Davies   Typical Pony Club high-flyer. 15 years old. Owns The Hawk, a 14.2 hh bay.

Judy Richards   Ash's head groom and sometime girlfriend. 18 years old.

Eric Burgess   Ash's uncle. Around 50 years old. His legs were paralysed in a riding accident. He has a basset hound called Daisy.

Look out for the definition-packed glossary of horsey terms at the back of the book.

CHAPTER ONE

"He's here!" Zoe burst through the tack room door, a head collar and lead rope trailing after her. "It's Joel, he's here. He's at the house!"

My boyfriend Ash came in after her. He was carrying two saddles, his gold-blonde hair sticking in tendrils to his neck, a rugby shirt hanging loose over suede jodhpurs. "He's only a trainer, for goodness' sake. Anybody would think he's the Prime Minister."

"Only a trainer?" Zoe looked aghast. "We're talking about Joel O'Ryan, champion three-day eventer, twice Badminton winner. How can you possibly say that?" Zoe wrinkled her freckled nose in disgust.

I was picking a marmite sandwich to pieces and feeding it to Nigel and Reggie, the stable ducks, who thought they were human and had their own blanket to sit on.

"Well come on, Alex." Zoe glared at me, defiant. "Don't tell me you're not just a teeny-weeny bit excited?"

Joel O'Ryan was an Irish trainer, in his late fifties, and was famous for discovering young riders and turning them into overnight stars. Of course I was excited – I'd thought of nothing else since the end of term. I was dying to know what he'd think of Barney.

"Well, if you ask me," Ash ran a tired hand over his unshaven chin, a needle edge to his voice, "there was no need to spend a packet on O'Ryan: Eric could have done the course just as well. He always was the better rider when they were young. It's a waste of Pony Club money."

Eric was Ash's uncle and my close friend. He'd turned Barney into a top class cross-country pony and promised to get me to the National Championships. But Ash didn't understand: Joel was famous, influential. He was here for a one-week training course at the Sutton Vale Pony Club. It was my big chance.

"You can do what you like but I'm well out of it." Ash pinched my can of Coke and drank half of it. "I've got six horses to ride single-handed and a new owner to show round, who" – he flicked up his wrist to examine his watch – "is precisely an hour late and no doubt an empty-headed time-waster."

"Hello?" Suddenly a blonde head poked round the glass door, having obviously overheard every single word. "I'm so sorry I'm late – my bicycle had a puncture." She hesitated and took in

2

Ash who looked decidedly icy, throwing back his head and draining the last of the Coke.

She was about fifteen with bleached cropped hair, tall and wearing the tightest pair of black Lycra shorts I'd ever seen.

"There's more fat on a pencil," Zoe whispered.

The girl was still taking in Ash, her slanty grey eyes examining his muscular shoulders and coming to rest on his perfectly curved, almost sullen mouth. A few months ago I'd have been raging with jealousy but experience had taught me to ignore smouldering glances. Basically I'd got used to every female over thirteen fancying him rotten.

"Ruth Hanson." The girl extended a golden brown, perfectly manicured hand. "I just can't wait to join your yard."

"I can't wait to join your yard." Zoe mimicked Ruth's tinkly voice as soon as she'd disappeared with Ash. "Why can't we get some decent owners for a change? You know, ones with a hint of personality?"

Zoe stuck her tongue out at her reflection in the old wall mirror and ruffled a hand through her sandy hair. "Yuck, I think I've aged ten years."

She'd just been sacked from a hairdressing salon for dying an old-age pensioner's hair orange when she should have been sweeping the floor. The final straw was when the manager caught her with her feet up watching the horse racing on a portable telly which ended up fusing the whole shop.

At fourteen Zoe was going through career options and being a female Nicky Clarke was now definitely off the list. The latest was physiotherapy for sportsmen, preferably footballers and famous tennis players, including Andre Agassi and Boris Becker. I didn't have a choice to make. I was going to be a famous three-day eventer. The next Mary King. Full stop.

Zoe started stumbling towards the door carrying three horse rugs, with a set of bandages wrapped round her neck. She could hardly see to walk.

"Where are you going?" I asked her.

"To the house of course." She stared at me as if I was stupid. "You might want to sit here drooling over pictures of William Fox-Pitt but I'm going to check out Joel O'Ryan."

Barney was out in the paddock with three other horses munching away at the sweet summer grass as if the moment he stopped it would all disappear. A chestnut mare was fluttering her eyelashes at him but he completely ignored her. Barney was a 14.2, tough, rugged dun. He had a mind of his own and was always getting into trouble. I blew him a kiss and ran on. I had to see Eric.

His cottage was in the parkland that was part of the Burgess estate. I cut through the wood and across the front lawn, noticing three plump mole-hills and a deckchair propped near the fish pond. Daisy flew out of the greenhouse as soon as she saw me. She jumped up, wiping her muddy paws all over my white jodhpurs and licking my hands. She was a brown and white basset hound with extra long ears – the most gorgeous dog I'd ever known.

Eric was in the greenhouse.

"So you finally got here then?" His grey head was bent low, his arm extended, gently trowelling at some clammy peat. He didn't look up once.

I plucked myself an over-ripe tomato and felt it squelch in my fingers. "Why didn't you tell me you knew Joel?"

The words hung in the air. I saw his neck stiffen. "I didn't realize it was any of your business."

Ouch, I wasn't prepared for that. He carried on digging, methodically, defensively, ignoring my presence.

"Well maybe not," I mumbled, wounded. "But I thought we were friends, you know – friends tend to tell each other things. I didn't realize there was one rule for you and another rule for me. I thought—"

"That's enough." Eric spun round. "Look at

5

me, Alex. Take a good hard look. Do you really think I want someone like Joel to see me like this?"

I was stunned. I stared at the wheelchair as if for the first time. I never thought of Eric as disabled. He'd had a terrible riding accident three years ago which left him paralysed from the waist down. When I first met him he used to have panic attacks if he was away from the cottage, but I thought he'd got over all that.

"Have you any idea what it's like to have to look up at people? To never be on the same eye level?"

I'd never seen him so full of bitterness. He reached down and pulled the blanket over his wasted legs. "Let's face the facts for once, Alex. I'm a cripple."

"But Joel wouldn't see you like that. You can't hide away because you've lost the use of your legs."

"Oh listen to yourself. All it's been for weeks is Joel this, Joel that. What will Joel think? Well I have feelings too, you know. Alexandra Johnson doesn't have exclusive rights to emotion. And I won't be made a laughing stock, not by O'Ryan or anybody. I have my pride if nothing else."

"But that's not true. I care about you, you know I do."

"I know you care about Barney. I know you care about winning. God knows I taught you

6

enough about ambition. But there's a limit, Alex. You've got to keep your feet on the ground."

"But I don't understand. What are you trying to say?" I was trembling now, shivers of cold prickling my neck. I felt disorientated, out on a limb, as if unknowingly I'd stepped on something fragile.

A muscle flickered in Eric's cheek. It was ages before he finally spoke. "I'm just a stupid old man who doesn't want to let go. You're special, Alex. You've got an amazing talent, and so has Barney. All I'm saying is, don't be misguided. Don't ruin everything on a false promise."

I swallowed hard and bent down to pat Daisy. Anything to break the tension. "I'm not pulling out of this training course."

"Well then, do as you must, but take my warning." Eric bent forward, his eyes flecked with real concern. "This is one pal speaking to another." His hand rested on my arm. "Joel O'Ryan is not a man you can trust. And if anybody knows I do – he's not all he appears."

CHAPTER TWO

"He's fantastic!" Zoe was sounding off like a foghorn. "He's witty, he's laid-back, he's charming, charismatic."

It was the first day of the training course and my stomach was churning like a cement mixer.

"In fact I'd say he looks a bit like Robert Redford but smaller." As Zoe was always prone to exaggeration nobody took any notice.

Mrs Brayfield, the Pony Club secretary, was charging around trying to give everybody name tags, her cheeks puffed out with exasperation and her opaque tights ruffling round her ankles. Unfortunately the sticky-back plastic had lost its stick and tags were flying off in all directions. Mine fell in Barney's water which made the ink run and I ended up being called "Alan".

The Sutton Vale Pony Club was made up of a lot of very spoilt teenagers with wealthy parents and nothing better to do than pour money into expensive and highly unsuitable ponies. Everybody was always being thrown off, trodden on, or was simply not moving at all. We were the disgrace of the county but nobody gave a hoot.

Mrs Brayfield came over with a poorly written speech scribbled on blue paper which she handed to Zoe. "What do you think?" she gasped as Zoe started reading it.

"Appalling!" Jasper Carrington, the biggest flirt in the area, marched across leading a liver chestnut called Star. It was an ex-polo pony, and was weighed down with every gadget under the sun.

"Oh, terribly sorry, I thought we were talking about Zoe's new lipstick." He winked at me and gave Mrs Brayfield a big kiss on the cheek. "So just when are we going to meet the 'Jolly Joel'?"

I was determined to make a good impression. Barney was looking gorgeous, his mane perfectly laid on the right side and his muscles rippling. I gave him a quick rub over with the stable rubber and shook out his tail for the zillionth time.

Everybody was getting restless. Toukie, Jasper Carrington's girlfriend, was sprawled on the grass. She looked like a goddess in a pink shirt and jods and was idly picking at a daisy. She was complaining to Zoe that Jasper was a snogaholic and what did Zoe think about showing affection in public?

Jasper sneaked up behind and slid his arms round her waist. "Relationships are like sharks, darling. If they don't move forward they die."

"He's here!" one of the youngsters yelled out and shot off to open a gate.

A Land Rover bounced across a rutted track towards Mrs Brayfield, who was waving frantically. Joel O'Ryan leapt out of the passenger seat, stooped down, plucked a tulip from a flower tub and held it out to Mrs Brayfield with a dramatic flourish.

"See, I told you he was fantastic." Zoe led her grey pony Lace out of the stable and pulled down the stirrup. "This is going to be a laugh a minute, I sense it in my bones."

Barney was skittering about, mainly because I was so tense my joints were creaking. He was the only dun horse there and he looked sensational.

We were all asked to mount and line up so Joel could introduce himself. My knees were trembling so much Zoe had to give me a leg-up. I'd read so many times how Joel could take an average rider and turn them into a star overnight. He just seemed to have the knack of pressing the right buttons, getting the right results.

"Alex?" Zoe passed me my jumping whip, her voice suddenly edged with concern. Lace snuggled up to Barney and nibbled his neck. "Don't you think you're taking this too seriously? I mean, what happened to Eric? You always said he was your mentor."

11

I opened my mouth and shut it again and then concentrated on gathering up my reins.

"I mean, you have been getting a bit carried away, haven't you? Joel this, Joel that."

A sudden wave of irritation flooded through me. "You don't know what you're talking about," I sniped back. "Why don't you listen to yourself? 'Oh, Joel's so fantastic' – you're the one with the problem."

"Yes, but I thought horses were supposed to be fun." Zoe pushed Lace forward, away from Barney. "Not an obsession."

Zoe had this way of unwittingly being able to prick my conscience. Eric's words were still floating around in the back of my head. It was the second warning I'd had about Joel. And I obstinately refused to listen.

Everybody was forming a line and I deliberately tagged on to the end so that Barney would stand out more. Toukie was next to me on Candy and casually picking at her fingernails holding her reins like washing lines. I straightened my back and pushed down my heels just as Eric had shown me.

Mrs Brayfield was fluttering all over the place, a huge sun hat flopping into her eyes which was in danger of being devoured by a chocolate-coloured pony with big teeth. By the time Joel got to Toukie I was doubling up with butterflies.

Joel had sandy hair scraped in long strands

12

over his head. His eyes twinkled and darted all over the place and he never stopped talking, in a soft lazy drawl which had everybody enchanted. Even Toukie was flashing her extra best smile and being unusually pleasant.

"Name me three different martingales," he asked as he examined Toukie's bridle for dirt.

"Standing, running and Irish." I butted in and instantly regretted it.

Joel's eyes locked on mine with a hint of disapproval and surprise.

"And you are?"

"Alexandra Johnson."

"Ah, I see. Eric's protégée. That explains it."

His eyes were roving over Barney now like a hungry animal, a sudden interest stopping the flow of conversation. There had recently been an article in *Horse and Hound* about Eric and how he had discovered me. I could only presume that's how he knew. My heart soared because he'd remembered my name.

"Perhaps you'd like to give us a little display of your talents, Miss Johnson."

I moved off at a purposeful trot trying to hold Barney together – he was itching to put in a few bucks. We performed a couple of wobbly figures of eight and stilted transitions and I was painfully aware that the whole of the Sutton Vale Pony Club was watching. And Joel.

13

We had to do better. The wooden railings came into view, solid, upright, and clocking on for three foot. It was no ordinary fence. Even top eventers would probably think twice. In one fleeting second I threw caution to the wind and turned towards it.

I could feel the hush of tension behind me. Someone shouted out a warning but it was muffled. We were five strides out. Barney hesitated, not really believing I was asking him to jump it.

"Come on, boy, don't let me down." His muscles bunched and his hind legs thrust underneath him.

Three, two – "Go on!" He snapped up his forelegs, skewered to one side and slithered over. It wasn't particularly stylish but we got over. We'd shown guts and tenacity. What every top rider needs.

I trotted back to the group with my cheeks burning and my hair all over the place. Mrs Brayfield was rigid with shock. Joel was expressionless, but for a nerve twitching in his cheek, and his hands pushed down hard into his pockets.

"Very spectacular," he said in an understated way. Then without warning he broke into a grin, quite unable to hide his excitement. "Atta boy Barney, atta boy." He thumped his neck and pulled his ears with new-found affection.

We'd done it. We'd caught the attention of Joel O'Ryan.

The rest of the morning was spent tackling a hectic succession of jumps. Everybody was pushed to the limit. Zoe rode over on Lace, her face flushed with exhilaration. "Did you see what I've just jumped?" she squeaked. "He's incredible. He just tells you to go for it, and you do."

Everybody was buzzing on a highly-charged wave of adrenalin. Sweaty ponies were galloping by, tackling cross-country fences as if they'd got wings. Usually in Eric's training sessions we spent three quarters of the time doing flatwork and then complicated exercises over small fences. Joel had everyone jumping massive fences. He just seemed to fill them with confidence.

"Well, if it isn't Alexandra the Great on her wonder horse, or is it Pegasus?" Jasper rode up trying to look "cool" with his riding hat swinging from the saddle. His tawny brown hair was slicked back, wet with sweat.

Toukie was giggling hysterically at his ever-ongoing flow of jokes.

"You know, Toukie, when I first met you, I thought to myself, she's wonderful, she laughs at everything I say. It took me quite a while to realize that you laugh at anything."

Toukie's face drained stark white and she cringed with embarrassment.

15

"Oh for God's sake, Jasper," I snapped. "Act your age, not your shoe size."

By the time we broke off for lunch everybody was exhausted. We sprawled out on the grass rucking up the Pony Club T-shirts to expose our midriffs. It was boiling hot, almost hazy, with a clear blue sky. I attacked a pile of cheese and tomato sandwiches. Zoe was lying flat-out saying she'd never be able to walk again.

Some of the junior Pony Clubbers were hovering around collecting money for a good cause. Mrs Brayfield came across with a trayful of plastic cups containing extra-diluted orange squash. I was so thirsty I could have drunk from a bucket.

Joel was in the Pony Club caravan no doubt having sandwiches with the crusts cut off and a cup of fresh tea. Everybody was singing his praises. I lay back on the grass and felt the sun warm my eyelids. Zoe suddenly leapt up saying she'd got ants in her pants and started attacking the ground with my can of Extra Tail fly spray.

I was just about to go back to sleep when Mrs Brayfield let out a nervous cough and said, "Oh look, it's Mr Burgess."

My eyes flew open and I sat bolt upright. The green Fiesta was parked slap bang next to the caravan. It was Eric.

It took him ages to get out of the car, to arrange his wheelchair in the right place and lever himself into it from the driving seat. I didn't go across straight away because I knew it would embarrass him. If there was one thing Eric hated it was people making a fuss. Unfortunately Mrs Brayfield wasn't so tactful.

Joel came down the caravan steps just as I sauntered across. Mrs Brayfield was flapping and insisting on pushing Eric's chair which was making him cringe. It couldn't have been a worse scenario. And I was caught right in the middle of it.

Joel did a double take and then held out his hand. "Eric, my old mate, how are you?" He grabbed Eric's hand and pumped it up and down. "Heard about the old pins and I'm terribly sorry, I should have been in touch."

"Enough of the flannel, O'Ryan. I don't need your sympathy."

Joel's smile deadened a little. "I see you're just as sharp as ever," he laughed.

"And you're still laying on the blarney." Eric stared him out. I noticed he was wearing his best shirt and tie and his hair was meticulously arranged. The tension between them was incredible.

"I think I'll leave you to it." Mrs Brayfield dived off in a flurry of flowery voluminous dress.

"Well, we should get together and catch up on old times." Joel looked as if he was stepping on egg shells. "Here's your little star." He held an arm out to me. "I'll have her cracking in no time, mark my words."

Despite the heat I was suddenly frozen and felt empty and dead inside. I couldn't meet Eric's eyes. I felt like a tennis ball being bandied back and forth between two players.

Eric looked away, his eyes full of hurt. I knew it looked as if I was turning my back on him but I couldn't help it. I couldn't stop myself. Besides, I wasn't doing anything wrong. I was just enjoying a one-week training course with the Pony Club. So what? Big deal. Eric was still my trainer.

"Anyway, must get back to it." Joel fidgeted uncomfortably and broke away.

Jasper Carrington was just coming back from the portable loos with one of the Bevan brothers and took in the whole scene. His vicious aside was all too audible.

"He's so old and prickly he could be a cactus," he smirked. "No wonder old Brayfield brought in Joel rather than him."

"Eric, no, don't go. He's an idiot, don't take any notice of him." Eric was wheeling frantically back to his car.

"Leave me alone, Alex. You've made your bed, now you can lie in it."

"You're being unreasonable." I was close to tears. "It's as if you're jealous. Eric, please, this is stupid. You're still my trainer."

"Save it, Alex. I'm not interested. And if you ever feel like visiting, don't bother."

"Eric!"

He slammed the car door shut right in my face. I banged on the window but he stubbornly ignored me. "Eric!"

All the Pony Clubbers were watching and nudging each other.

"Eric!" My voice was out of control.

He drove off in a series of fits and jerks and I was just left standing there alone, like an idiot. I knew Joel's eyes were burning into my back. I was suddenly engulfed with a gnawing sense of guilt and loneliness.

There on the ground, half hidden in the clover, was a crumpled photograph. I stooped down and picked it up, cradling it in both hands. It must have fallen out of Eric's pocket as he got into the car in a rush. It was black and white and a lovely blonde-haired girl in a summer dress stared out at me. Who was she? A man in top hat and tails was standing next to her, an arm round her shoulder. They looked so much in love. On the back were scrawled the words: "To Tanya with love."

I didn't have to read it twice. I was one hundred per cent sure. It was Eric's handwriting.

CHAPTER THREE

"Who's Tanya?" Zoe yanked down the ramp on the trailer and we led Lace and Barney into their respective stables.

It was eight o'clock at night and the training course had only just finished. Barney looked shattered and could hardly wait for me to take off his travelling gear. Zoe's mum said she was just popping off to the all-night shop and would be back in half an hour. I mixed up some horse nuts, oats, chaff and sliced carrots and watched Barney tuck in with a vengeance. Nigel was cleaning his feathers over by the water bucket and refused to vacate the stable until I gave him a handful of oats. I was so exhausted I could hardly stand up straight. Luckily someone had already bedded down and filled Barney's hay net so all I had to do was settle him for the night. Zoe said if I got any more bags under my eyes I'd have a full set of luggage.

"So just who is this mystery Tanya?"

The photograph was still in my jodhpur pocket, pressed close and safe. Obviously she had been his girlfriend but Eric had never mentioned her name. Until today I'd never imagined Eric to have ever been in love with anyone.

"Feathers are going to fly between those two, mark my words." Zoe wagged her finger. "I've never seen two men hate each other so much."

I had an uncomfortable feeling she was right.

"God, what's happened here?" We pushed open the tack room door to be met by a complete mess. Rugs, bandages, back protectors, a double bridle slewn across the floor. A huge wicker basket was just dumped in the doorway.

"Where on earth has all this come from?"

"I can explain."

Ash was suddenly behind us, hands on hips, still in his riding chaps, his whole body vibrating with energy and enthusiasm.

"W-what?"

"Don't say a word." He grabbed my arm and then Zoe's and almost frogmarched us across to the stables.

"I couldn't believe it," he tried to explain, excitement making his voice deep and husky. "I could hardly control myself and she was so blasé, as if it's an everyday occurrence owning a horse that's qualified for Badminton."

"Ash, what are you talking about?"

He slapped a hand over my eyes, pulled back a stable bolt, pushed me through the door, and then, whispering very gently in my ear, his breath warm and tickling, said, "Look at that!"

Zoe gasped at my side. I took a step back and fell into Ash's arms.

"Oh Ash, he's beautiful." We were staring at a sensational dapple grey, about 16.3 hands, with the most incredible black mane and tail. He was all muscle and perfectly proportioned. In fact he was the most perfect horse I'd ever seen.

"You are now looking at the priceless property of our new livery owner." Ash kissed me on the cheek and lifted a hand to the grey's broad neck. "Ruth Hanson."

"What, that straggly string bean with the Lycra shorts owns a horse like this?" I was completely gobsmacked. "He's fantastic."

"She, actually. Her name's Sunshine Girl and she's ten years old. She used to belong to an Australian who went broke. Ruth bought her three days ago."

Patsy, Zoe's mum, blasted on the horn from the Land Rover Discovery and Zoe said she'd have to dash. Ash promised to give me a lift home.

"See you tomorrow, seven o'clock," Zoe shouted, running backwards. "And don't forget to have an Epsom salts bath."

Sunshine Girl pricked up her ears and nuzzled me in the ribs.

"Don't you see?" Ash ran a hand through his blonde hair, more relaxed now that we were alone.

23

"She's an advanced event horse – if I can talk Ruth into giving me the ride it could be my ticket to stardom. This horse has got something. It stands out a mile off."

"But how do you know she's looking for a rider?" I was trying to take it all in. "Surely she'll want to compete herself?"

"She's been riding six months and she's completed a minimus. She doesn't know a browband from a martingale. We're quids in, Alex. We've got it made." He twirled me off my feet, euphoria taking over. "If Donavon qualifies too I could have two rides at the biggest championships in the world. Eat your heart out, William Fox-Pitt."

I'd never seen him so elated. He gave me a kiss and ruffled my hair. Sunshine Girl wrinkled up her top lip and did an impression of a camel.

"But you've still got to convince Ruth," I said, and somehow, remembering those slanty grey eyes, I didn't think she'd exactly be a pushover.

"Trust me." Ash wrapped his arms tight round my waist. "I've got it sussed."

We climbed into his American jeep. I curled up my legs in the front seat, throwing two riding hats into the back. A rosette dangled from the wing mirror and a sticker was peeling off the windscreen saying "Slow Down For Horses". I could have gladly gone to sleep there and then.

Ash started giving me a rundown on the day's

performance of all six of his eventers. From who did a flying change to George putting in a stop at a triple spread. This was a way of life for professional horsey people; they lived and breathed horses and I couldn't imagine any other existence. To me it was heaven.

I gossiped away about Joel, totally missed out the episode with Eric and tried to gradually bring the conversation round to Tanya. If anybody knew the lie of the land Ash would, but he always clammed up whenever we talked about Eric's past. He changed the subject by talking about what to wear for an upcoming photo shoot: his leather flying jacket or a polo shirt, jodhpurs or chaps, cowboy hat or baseball cap?

I spotted Eric's car in the mini-supermarket car park mainly because I was looking out for it. He always did his weekly shopping late on a Monday evening because it was the quietest time of the week. He hated having to fight the weekend crowds down the aisles – mothers, toddlers and trolleys.

"I'm hungry," I said.

Ash followed my instructions, swerved into the right-hand lane and jolted into the car park.

"Here," I said, fishing out a horsey crossword. "Entertain yourself for five minutes. I won't be long."

"Oh and Alex?" I was just about to close the door when Ash spoke. "I'll have two king-sized

Mars Bars and a packet of Worcester sauce crisps . . . And don't cause a scene with Eric."

I blushed and stomped off towards the trolleys. I thought I'd got him fooled.

A gaggle of teenage boys burst through the electric doors laughing their heads off at something, one ripping open a packet of peanuts which cascaded everywhere.

I barged past, ignoring the stupid jokes about tight jodhpurs and boots and where had I left my horse. My only interest was finding Eric. Two cash-till assistants stopped gossiping and gave me wary looks. I rushed past the baked beans and canned soups, well aware that it would soon be time for closing. The bright fluorescent lights felt harsh even though it was still light outside.

I very nearly knocked over a display of washing powder trying to squeeze past some shoppers. Then inspiration struck. I headed straight for the sign saying Pet Foods and there he was.

He was reading the back of a box of dog biscuits, his lips pursed with concentration, furrows lining his forehead. Trust Daisy's food to get the most attention. All that was in his trolley was a pile of tinned vegetables, potatoes and baked beans.

"I think she'd prefer wholewheat flavour myself." I looked down at him, praying that he was in a softer mood. "There's something you dropped, something I need to return to you." I pulled out the

26

photograph and handed it to him. I could sense his embarrassment.

A shelf stacker walked past smiling warmly as if it was good to see a teenager helping the elderly. I scowled back and noticed the photograph had disappeared under Eric's blanket.

"Well, are you pleased to see me?" It was a stupid thing to say, especially in a supermarket, but I couldn't stand the strain.

"You shouldn't have come." Eric moved on, turning his back, wheeling over to the meat counter. "I suppose that old mothball O'Ryan sent you."

I reached inside the freezer and picked out some minced beef he couldn't quite reach. "That's rubbish and you know it."

"Well now you've got your fancy new trainer I'd have thought you'd have been tucked up in bed. Reciting his words of wisdom. O'Ryan likes results no matter what."

"Why are you being so nasty?" My hands were trembling from the cold of the minced beef and I slung it in the trolley a little too violently. "I think you're jealous," I hissed, wanting to shake him. Anything to bring him to his senses. "I think you're feeling left out and you're wallowing in self-pity." I had a habit of being too blunt and out-spoken – once the words were out there was no way of raking them back in.

Eric looked horrified. "There you go again

27

blasting off at the mouth." His voice was almost a whisper. I'd really blown it this time.

"See if this rings any bells ... 'Alex, I think you've got the talent to get right to the top. I'm prepared to take you on as a pupil, but you have to push Barney harder. He needs more experience. Why put off the chance of glory until next year when you can have it now?' Am I right? Do I have a point?"

He'd just repeated the speech which Joel had made to me when the others had gone. It was almost word perfect. My jaw nearly dropped open but some inner pride locked my features in place. "I don't know what you're talking about."

"Oh, Alex. It's written all over your face. He's sucked you in, hook, line and sinker."

"He has not." My voice was rising to a startled screech. We were collecting quite an audience.

"Come back to me when you've seen some sense. And for Barney's sake, don't leave it too long." Eric wheeled purposefully down the aisle towards the cash tills.

I was left clutching some vanilla-flavoured biscuits feeling a right fool. I suddenly remembered that I'd forgotten to ask him about Tanya. I'd been completely sidetracked. I could just see his grey head bobbing through the electric doors. Drat, drat, drat. Why did he always end up making me feel so bad?

"A message for Miss Alexandra Johnson.

Could she please hurry up with the chocolate as her boyfriend is passing out with hunger." Some of the staff giggled. That was Ash's idea of a joke – he'd no doubt charmed one of the girls into broadcasting the message. He could charm the birds out of the trees when he put his mind to it.

Brick-red with embarrassment, I had a good mind to take him the dog biscuits. By the time I got back to the jeep he was pretending to doze with the crossword page over his face.

"Monster," I shouted, scrunching up my face.

"Well, you made a fine mess of that one." He switched on the ignition. "So my uncle Eric is wallowing in self-pity, is he?" He burst into laughter.

"You pig," I howled. "You were listening."

"Standing at the other side of the pet foods actually. You do sound gorgeous when you're steamed up."

We were halfway down the road before I stopped hitting him with the crossword magazine.

An hour soaking in an Epsom salts bath until my skin had shrivelled like a prune did not make me feel any better. I had just finished studying a dressage test for the next day, chanting out the slogan, All King Edward's Horses Call Men Blooming Fools. If you took the first letter from each word it gave you the dressage marker letters in the correct order. It was the only way I could remember. I now had this month's copy of *In The Saddle* propped up by the soap dish and was trying to memorize "coffin canter" – a slow bouncy canter with lots of impulsion. I had to try and impress Joel by at least knowing my way around a cross-country course and the difference between a bullfinch and a steeplechase. My future career depended on it.

The bubble bath was just starting to fizz away to nothing when I heard the pounding on the front door. Someone was rattling the door knocker as if their life depended on it. We lived on a mock Tudor estate where nothing ever happened. I could imagine curtains twitching right around the close.

The front door opened and clicked shut and I heard my mother shout up the stairs. "Alex – it's Ash for you."

Water splattered everywhere as I jumped out, grabbed a towel and dashed into my bedroom to make myself decent. My very worst fear was something happening to Barney. Ash coming to tell me the news, being sympathetic, saying it couldn't be helped. Please God, don't let it be Barney.

Heart hammering like a steam engine I threw on a dressing gown and galloped down the stairs. Ash was in the hallway, his face grey, wringing his hands as my mother offered him a cup of tea.

Something terrible had happened, I knew it.

"It's Eric." Ash could hardly speak. "He's collapsed – he's in hospital!"

CHAPTER FOUR

Mum dropped me off at the hospital the next morning.

It was apparently a stress attack. The doctors were pretty sure it wasn't his heart. Guilt gnawed away at me like woodworm. If only I hadn't gone off at the deep end. If I hadn't upset him . . .

"You can see him now." A nurse with Titian red hair smiled warmly and showed me the way. I was clutching a bedraggled bunch of flowers and some grapes. That nauseating clinical hospital smell was making me feel claustrophobic.

I saw Ash and his parents before I saw Eric. He was grey and lifeless and totally uninterested in what anyone had to say. He just lay there, propped up on three pillows, pleating the bedspread.

"Oh Eric, I never meant for this to happen," I said.

"Um, we're just off to the canteen." Mr Burgess shuffled his wife and Ash away from the bed. "Give you two some time to talk."

Ash put a hand on my arm. "I'll bring you a coffee," he whispered, his face strained.

A man in the next bed was listening and

watching even though he was pretending to read the paper.

"Mr Burgess says you'll need lots of rest." I pulled up a chair and placed the flowers and grapes on the side table next to some Lucozade.

"I should put those out of sight, love." The man in the next bed started guffawing. "There's a mystery grape-snatcher in the ward. I'm sure it's the sister."

Eric's face hardened and the man buried himself back in the paper.

"How's Daisy?" It was Eric's first question.

Ash had left her with me for the night while they went to the hospital. The poor thing had whimpered all night. She'd never been away from Eric before, not since she was a puppy. I'd given her a hot-water bottle, warmed her some rice pudding, and sat cuddling her until three o'clock in the morning.

"She's fine," I gulped. "She's chewed up my slippers and all my Frankie Sloothaak posters."

"You never could lie very well." Eric was on to me like a shot.

"What's the food like?" I desperately tried to change the subject.

"Why aren't you riding?" he asked.

"Some things are more important." Tears welled up and began to trickle down the side of my nose.

"Now don't start blubbing. Come on, girl, you know I can't stand it when you cry."

"I can't help it, I feel so bad." I grabbed the bedspread and mopped frantically at my eyes.

"Alex, for heaven's sake, lighten up. I'm not dead yet."

The nurse came round and asked if everything was all right. "I've still got a pulse if that's what you mean." Eric grinned and tapped me across the head. "Pull yourself together, you silly mare. You're embarrassing me."

"But I feel so guilty."

"A useless emotion if ever there was one. Now dry your face. I've got something to tell you."

I sat back in the chair, trembling like a whippet, taking deep breaths.

"I'm not going to snuff it, so you don't have to worry about a funeral, but there's not much left in me, Alex. You're going to have to find yourself a new trainer."

My heart lurched. "But you can't mean it – we need you!"

"Look at me. I'm hardly a Mike Tyson, am I? No, I've made my decision, and you know I'm immovable when I've set my mind on something."

"I don't believe you." Horror and a gnawing emptiness washed over me. "You can't give in. I won't let you."

"Now don't carry on. I'll still help you, but I'm too old to be trailing all over the country."

"That's not true." I was sniffing now, short stilted sobs rasping my throat.

Eric passed me a box of tissues.

"You'll have to respect my decision, Alex."

"I will not," I sniffed.

"Just promise me one thing." Eric leant forward. "Don't get involved with Joel."

Suddenly a bustling nurse took over, propping him up on the pillows, reaching for equipment, telling him to be quiet.

"Look after Daisy," Eric shouted after me, a hint of desperation in his voice. And then the nurse was pulling the green clinical curtain round the bed and I was left standing by myself in the middle of the ward, red-eyed and trembling, every patient's eyes riveted on me.

"Are you all right, dear?" An elderly lady with a blue rinse caught my arm as I scuttled through reception in a daze.

I looked down into her watery blue eyes and thought of my grandmother. "No, I don't think I am," I croaked, half falling into a plant display and feeling chilled to the marrow.

She plonked me down on a plastic seat, brought me a cup of tea, and waited until I'd pulled myself together.

It was ages before I found my way back to the

stable yard. The old lady paid for a taxi and it was only as I was leaving the hospital grounds that I remembered Ash and his promised cup of coffee.

The taxi driver tried to jolly me up with an endless stream of jokes but I just wanted to crawl into a hole and die. For the last six months I'd lived and breathed eventing and now it seemed the most unimportant thing in the world.

"Cheer up, beautiful. It can't be that bad," said the driver as I climbed out of the taxi, and saw Zoe dragging a huge hay net into Lace's stable, Daisy plodding after her.

Ash was by the car door in an instant, his tall frame leaning over. He must have left the hospital ages ago. "What happened to you?" He tried to hide his irritation. "You completely disappeared!"

I wandered over to Barney's stable desperate to stroke his neck and bury my head in his long mane.

"Alex, will you come back." Ash loped after me. "He's not in there any more."

Sunshine Girl put her grey head over the door, shook herself from head to foot, and dropped hay all down my shoulder.

"Where's Barney?" I yelped. "This is his stable."

"Apparently Sunny likes a stable pointing south, and this was always too big for Barney. I knew you'd understand."

I glared at him.

"Barney's round the back . . ."

"In the piggery?" I was furious.

"The converted stables." Ash narrowed his eyes to sapphire slits. "I am the boss round here, you know – a detail you seem to continually overlook."

"Yes, sir." I clipped my heels together and saluted, wondering whether it was possible to love and hate someone at the same time.

"Don't be so obnoxious," Ash hissed under his breath. He always used big words when he wanted to put me down. "You know I'm trying to get in with Ruth."

"Does that include her bra?" I closed my eyes with regret as soon as the words left my lips. Ash blazed with anger and I thought he was going to shake me.

"You really push people to the limit, do you know that?" He turned on his heel and stormed off towards the outdoor manege.

Daisy rushed over delighted to see me and stuck a sloppy nose in my hand. "Oh darling, who needs boyfriends?" I bent down and hugged her soft chubby body, and decided in half a second that animals were far preferable to any human company.

"We're going to this party whether you like it or not – and we're taking Ruth." Ash was still in a raging bad mood and stalking up and down in the common room where we'd arranged to meet. It was joined on to the stable block and had every amenity from a pool table to a fridge. I bent down and offered Daisy a fresh bowl of water but she just looked at me with huge doleful eyes.

"Can't you see you're upsetting Daisy?" I offered her another sausage roll but she wouldn't touch it.

We were supposed to be going to Jasper Carrington's sixteenth birthday party. Ash only wanted to go because Jasper's dad was talking about moving his polo ponies to his yard. Even worse, we had to pick up Ruth on the way.

Zoe burst through the door in multi-coloured leggings and a cropped top. She was very late and explained she'd got carried away watching recordings of *Animal Hospital*.

"Can we please go now?" Ash grabbed the car keys and made for the door.

"Well, if you insist on taking Ruth" – I stood up – "I'm taking Daisy!"

We fell out of the jeep outside the Carrington mansion and Daisy's lead immediately got wrapped round my legs. Ruth had complained all the way because I'd insisted on having all the windows down for Daisy. Ash had given me a black look in the rear-view mirror when I suggested she wear more clothes.

Fairy lights were strung up in all the trees and the party already looked well under way. Two pony clubbers I vaguely recognized were racing round the flower beds with a hose pipe. Ruth complained her stiletto heels were sinking into the lawn and Zoe commented that she was probably beheading hundreds of worms. I was suddenly engulfed with a great wave of loneliness.

The music was blasting out full volume and as Ash opened the door Toukie nearly fell straight through it. "Oh terribly sorry," she hiccuped. "Oh what a novel idea bringing a dog – is it a prezzie for Jasper?"

If I could have picked Daisy up and clung to her I would have done. Instead I just shot Toukie an arctic look.

Jasper appeared clutching three glasses, his eyes immediately roving all over Ruth's svelte figure. "Nice skirt, sweetie. It'll be fantastic when it's finished."

I burst out laughing as Ruth gingerly pulled it down an inch in an attempt to make it more decent.

"I wouldn't bother, darling. You look sensational." Jasper swayed dangerously and I instantly regretted being talked into coming. I was in no mood for a wild party, especially with the Sutton Vale crew.

A girl called Anna and nicknamed Spanner shot past in a swimming costume shrieking her head off and ran through the open patio doors.

Zoe and I avoided the main bustle and headed across to the food and drinks. Daisy pressed up against my ankle and tried to disappear under the tablecloth.

Zoe poured out two glasses of a weird-looking punch in a washing-up bowl with fruit floating in the middle. On second thoughts we decided to have some of the fruit juice set out in a crystal jug.

"God, this is a nightmare." Zoe looked round in blatant disapproval.

"We'll leave early," I resolved, wanting to go straight away.

We browsed through some birthday cards set out on the mantelpiece, just for something to do. One was signed "My Peachbum from Popeye" and another "To Pancake from Tiny. Love you always."

"He probably writes them to himself just so he looks popular." Zoe filled a paper plate to the ceiling. "Oh God, don't look now, but Joel's turned up. He must be the only adult here."

I dived under the table and fed Daisy a plate of sausages. I was still stinging from Eric's words of rejection at the hospital. Even worse, I'd rung up later to see how he was and the nurse said he refused to talk to anybody and he didn't want any visitors. I felt cut to the quick.

Four glasses of supposed orange juice later, I felt as if my head was suffering a minor earthquake. Zoe had a glazed look and was chattering to a boy with watercress stuck in his front teeth who kept telling her she looked like a million dollars.

I decided to take Daisy for a walk round the grounds to clear my head. I was feeling so lonely I was having to fight back tears. I hadn't seen Ash all night and even outside there were couples kissing everywhere. I just wanted to go home.

"Hey, come on." Toukie grabbed my arm. "You're missing the snogging competition."

We went back into the house together with me resolving to find Ash and insist he take me home. I didn't have to look very far.

There was a crescendo of table thumping, whistles and yahooing and there sitting on Ash's knee was Ruth trying to kiss him.

Breathless with hurt I raced out again, stumbled over to the nearest tree and collapsed in a heap sobbing my heart out. I felt as if a hundred knives were stabbing into my chest, exposing raw one hundred per cent proof jealousy. I knew Ruth was trouble. She was too nice, too smarmy, altogether too false. Daisy cuddled into my shoulder, licking my face, whimpering and trembling.

"Oh sweetheart, we've both been deserted." A fresh cascade of tears ran down my face mixing with mascara, so when I wiped my cheek my hand was stained black.

"Trust me not to wear waterproof." I sniffed loudly. I pulled at the scrunchie tying up my hair and let it unfold in blond swathes round my neck. "I bet I look like Patsy from *Absolutely Fabulous*," I gulped. "Only she's a zillion times more glamorous."

That's when the dam burst and I was consumed with huge racking sobs.

I didn't hear the person coming towards me. I was only aware of another presence when a huge hanky was thrust down at me.

"Good Lord, if you carry on like that you won't be able to see for a week."

I was reminded of Eric. My eyes already felt like two mini-airships. They always ballooned when I had a heavy-duty cry.

"It's just not fair," I gulped and then hiccuped, clutching at Daisy. "Why is it always me who gets dumped on?"

The silhouette in front of me started laughing loudly, not showing the slightest trace of sympathy. I blew my nose. "No matter how hard I try everything always goes wrong."

He stopped laughing and squatted down on his knees. "The things most worth having cause us the most pain."

I felt like asking him how he'd got so knowledgeable, but instead I bit my bottom lip and squinted at him.

I should have recognized the soft lilting drawl. Joel's eyes shone out of the darkness, crinkling at the edges with amusement.

"How would you really like to get back at Ash and Ruth?" Joel's eyes were dancing like fireflies. "The best way to mend a broken heart is to fight back."

All that spiked orange juice was making my head spin. I tried to hold myself perfectly still but the ground was still moving.

"How would you like to go to Sweden?"

I nearly choked with shock. It was the last thing I was expecting.

"I really can't afford a holiday. It's very sweet of you, but I'm sorry."

"It's to ride, you idiot. On a team. With Barney."

I slowly raised my head, my jaw dropping as he stared at me with a dead-set, utterly serious, no-messing-about expression.

"You mean, competing abroad?" I squeaked.

"You've got what it takes, Alex. You're wasted here in the backwaters. Let's put you in the spotlight, make the selectors go crazy. You can do it, I know you can."

"Well, um, I don't know."

"All expenses paid. Come on, Alex, don't turn down the opportunity of a lifetime. Use your head."

At that moment I was having enough problems coping with getting my words out in the right order to even contemplate leaving the country. Somewhere in my brain Eric's words of warning jumbled together and then slowly disintegrated.

What was I worried about? What would anyone care anyway? Eric and Ash had abandoned me, and where was Zoe in my hour of need? No, I had to think about myself, me and Barney.

Joel smiled reassuringly. "There's not much time – I'll have to phone through your name tomorrow." He examined his fingernails with concentrated intensity. "You see, there are three other candidates."

Disappointment suddenly lurched in my stomach. "No, no, it's OK, I'll go. Sweden here I come." My voice rose with false bonhomie. "After all" – I squeezed Daisy tighter, my senses reeling, "what have I got to lose?"

CHAPTER FIVE

"So you really want to go to Sweden?" Zoe tied Lace up next to Barney, still trying to absorb what I'd just been telling her.

"It's the opportunity of a lifetime," I repeated mechanically for the hundredth time. "I'd be a fool not to take it."

"So why do you look so miserable then?"

I was standing on a bucket trying to plait up Barney who kept shaking his head every time I approached with the needle and thread. Joel had insisted that everybody plait up properly but with my head still throbbing from last night all I could produce was a mass of fat wispy golf balls.

"I'm not miserable." I rethreaded the needle. "I'm just subdued."

Zoe angled me one of her no-nonsense, straight to the point looks. Dressed in jodhpurs, Doc Martens and her brother's sweatshirt, she appeared, as usual, slightly eccentric, but she was the most practical person I'd ever known.

"Well, if you ask me it's complete madness, and it doesn't add up. I can smell a shipful of rats a mile off."

I was just about to ask her what she meant when Camilla Davies, one of the livery owners, rushed across complaining that Daisy had just wolfed the whole of her packed lunch and asking if somebody could please tell her what cow hocks meant because Joel would go for the jugular if she didn't find out. Cam had already plaited The Hawk so Joel had given her some horsey terms to learn.

"And what in Dickens' name is a ewe neck and a roach back? Good heavens, Alex, are you all right? You look awful."

Immaculate and as glamorous as ever, Cam always had a way of making me feel bug-eyed and infinitely ugly.

"If I see a frog I'll make sure I kiss it," I reassured her with a weak smile and disappeared under Barney's neck.

"This is all to do with Ash, isn't it?" Zoe hissed as I scrabbled on the ground for the plastic mane comb. Camilla disappeared in a flurry of blonde hair and pillar-box red lipstick intent on finding a horse dictionary.

The mere thought of Ash made me physically wince. I was rigid with anger and jealousy and had spent the whole night thinking up methods of medieval torture.

"There's no accounting for taste in men," Zoe snorted. "But honestly, Alex, you've got to have the worst in history."

"Quite frankly my dear," I pulled myself up Barney's shoulder, my throat parched and my knees knocking, "if I never saw the cheating rat-bag louse ever again I wouldn't care."

"Well, brace yourself." Zoe looked straight past me. "Because talk of the devil, he's just walked into the yard."

"You completely overreacted." Ash leaned against the wall, his legs stretched out, one heel lazily kicking the other.

I tried to ignore the way the sun was filtering through his hair highlighting the honey streaks and concentrated instead on scraping the horse grease from under my fingernails.

"She just leapt on me as soon as I sat down. I don't fancy her at all. In fact, it was more like being kissed by a sink plunger. Honestly Alex, you've got to believe me."

He turned on his puppy dog expression which he knew always melted my heart. "You do believe me, don't you? What kind of relationship do we have if there's no trust?"

I bit down hard on my bottom lip and tried to control the swirling emotions of hurt and confusion.

"It's you I love." He clasped my right hand and squeezed it tightly. "We're like two peas in a pod, you know that."

47

"Well . . ." I hesitated. "I suppose she was a bit full on."

"Like a steam train," Ash grinned.

"Rampant Ruth," I giggled.

"That's better." He kissed my forehead which I prayed wasn't too sweaty. "Now the thing is, Sunshine Girl is even better than I first thought." His voice rose with excitement. "Ruth has guaranteed me the ride but she wants me to be her boyfriend. I thought maybe I could pretend for a few weeks, just until my name's on the entry list. It wouldn't be for long. What do you think? Alex?"

I was furious. In one split second I dived off the wall, grabbed the hosepipe, yanked on the tap and blasted it straight at Ash with no mercy.

"You rat!" I screeched. "You miserable, conniving worm." I put my thumb halfway over the nozzle so the water sprayed out in an ice-cold jet.

"Alex, stop it, you idiot!" Water dripped everywhere, his shirt was drenched. I then concentrated on ruining his two hundred pound pair of suede jods. "Alex, stop it!"

"You've got as much depth as a puddle, Burgess," I yelled, wanting to wrap the hosepipe round and round his neck.

"*Alex, stop it!*" Zoe suddenly turned off the tap, her face twisted with tension.

The hosepipe fell out of my hand and my anger drained away as quickly as the water.

Zoe looked shellshocked. "That was the hospital on the phone." She stumbled for words and then went on. I hadn't even heard the phone ring. "Eric checked himself out this morning. Nobody knows where he's gone. There's no easy way to put this, but he's completely disappeared!"

Half an hour later, we were no closer to knowing where Eric had gone.

"He wouldn't leave Daisy!" I was adamant about that.

"For heaven's sake, Alex, he's an old man who's gone walkabout. He probably doesn't even know what he's doing." Ash was stalking the tack room floor.

"He's not an old man," I screeched. "He's just feeling left out. He's lost his sense of purpose."

"If we could just find the taxi driver who took him from the hospital . . ." Zoe chewed her nails, trying to be logical.

"Just leave it with me," Ash said, then told us he'd ring round all of Eric's old friends. "If you don't get to that training session Joel will have your guts for garters. There's nothing more you can do."

"How we're expected to concentrate when Eric's gone AWOL I really haven't a clue," I said, tightening Barney's girth.

He was spinning round and round, snapping at the reins, snorting at the slightest shadow. I had hoof oil and grass stains all down my jods. The last thing I could concentrate on was riding like a professional. I just wanted to go back to the yard and track down Eric.

Toukie suddenly charged past looking green and heading in the direction of the toilets, a hand clasped over her mouth. Jasper followed at a more sedate pace with his riding hat on back to front and leading Star, his liver chestnut, who was as wound up as Barney.

"We've got to be out on the cross-country course in the next three minutes or else," he ordered, vaulting easily into the saddle and gathering up the reins like a cowboy. "Oh don't worry about her," he said to Zoe, as she stared towards Toukie's disappearing back. "She had triple helpings of cold custard and ice cream for breakfast."

"He must be out of his mind," said a fair-haired girl on a chubby cob. Joel was striding up and down in front of us trying to explain how to jump the most enormous log pile I'd ever seen.

"It's the size of a house," Zoe hissed, trying to get Lace to stand up straight.

Joel marched up and down, his hand movements going in all directions as he excitedly explained the best approach.

"You've got to stay straight. It's no good wafting all over the place, you've got to keep both

50

legs on and jump within six inches of the spot you aim for."

In the last session we'd spent a full hour cantering over a pole on the ground and jumping a particular point which Joel had marked with sticky tape. Apparently when horses came to jump complicated combinations like coffins and bounces it was all this basic training which paid off.

"You ask Ginny Elliot." Joel had shot one of the Bevan brothers down in flames. "It's accuracy which counts, time and again."

Joel suddenly examined his fingernails with his usual intensity. "Now Alex, I think it's time you showed off your talents."

"I can't jump that!" I said, my voice rattling out in a staccato quiver.

"Now now, come come." Joel gave me an impish grin. "There's no such word as 'can't', you surely know that." Thoughts of Sweden whizzed through my mind – anything to knock Ash down a peg or two.

"I'd rather be an Olympic slalom skier than jump that." Zoe was suddenly stoney white.

"Which is precisely why you haven't been asked." Joel strode across to the log pile and removed the red flag. "Over the hedge, turn in a wide arc and down over this. It's a doddle – anybody could do it. Now come on, we haven't got all day."

Barney moved forward obediently. I was riding on automatic pilot, my brain paralysed with fear.

"Good luck." Damian Bevan winked at me as I tightened my reins. "Rather you than me," he giggled. The girl on the chubby cob looked frightened to death.

"Oh God, Barney, it's all down to you." I stroked his neck and pushed him into canter. I suddenly felt very alone, detached from the group of riders huddled under the trees near the Land Rover, watching. Waiting. Well we weren't going to give them the satisfaction of failing.

"Come on, sweetheart. You can jump it, I know you can."

We powered forward towards the two foot nine hedge.

"Steady, boy, steady!" Up, over and down again. The perfect landing. Barney was eating up the ground, his ears flicking back and forth, listening to my every command. "Good boy, good boy, now keep your concentration." I turned towards the log pile which was about fifty strides out.

My head buzzed with Eric's warnings. "Never push your horse, never overface him." But how did you ever improve if you didn't reach for the stars?

"Whoa boy, whoa, you're going too fast." I sat back and took a pull, trying to find a line, trying

52

to keep straight. It was vital I kept my eye on the highest part of the jump to find a good stride. But Barney was getting faster and faster. My eyes were watering, the chin strap on my riding hat started flapping against my cheek.

I wasn't ready.

Barney just grabbed the bit and leapt into space.

"Barney!"

I felt his shoulder crack against the top log. He staggered, slithered, desperately squirming to keep his balance.

"Alex!" Zoe's voice rang out in my ears but there was nothing she could do – we were going to fall.

I crashed to the ground on my right hip and frantically tried to roll clear. Something hard and metal flew after me which I later realized was a stirrup.

The sickening thud was like nothing I'd ever heard.

Barney lay, sprawled on his side, his hoofs scrabbling the air. His coat was slicked with blood down one forearm and his eyes were rolling in panic.

"Oh my God, oh my God. Oh Barney!" Next thing Joel grabbed both my arms and dragged me away, his strength pulling me off my feet. "What are you trying to do, kill yourself? There's nothing you can do. Leave him!"

"Barney!" He wasn't neighing, he wasn't doing anything, just lying there, helpless.

"He's done for!" A voice filtered through, tight with fear.

"Do something," I screamed, blood dripping from my nose and mouth onto my clean shirt. "Don't you see," I glared at Joel, "he's broken his back!"

"You don't know that!"

"It's all right, baby, it's all right." I crouched down by his neck, running my fingers over and over his soft silky mane. "Sssh now, just lie still."

Joel undid the girth and let the saddle fall back onto the ground. Jasper had gone to fetch a vet. "He's not in any pain." Joel put a hand on my shoulder.

"Get away," I said savagely, flinching back. "This is all your fault, you've killed my boy. It's all your fault."

Zoe tried to lead me away. "No!" I flung my arm into her waist, pushing her off. "Leave me alone!"

"Alex, you're getting hysterical. That's not going to help Barney."

"*Give him space!*" The voice boomed out familiar and authoritative behind me.

"Eric!"

"For heaven's sake, girl, help me into this wheelchair quick. Don't just stand there."

Mrs Brayfield was behind the steering wheel of the car, tears welling up in the corner of her eyes. "Eric Burgess, you're not fit enough!"

"Enough of your blathering, woman. Now, how long has he been like this?"

"Five minutes." Joel marched up, panic creeping into his voice. "It looks bad."

"He's trying to get up!" Zoe stepped back.

"Stay away! Keep away from those legs!"

Barney struggled, his sides heaving, and then lay back, gasping.

"He's going to die!" The girl with the blonde hair threw herself into Mrs Brayfield's arms, distraught.

"Poppycock." Eric banged the arm of his wheelchair. "He's winded, any clown can see that."

"I think you're wrong." Joel folded his arms across his chest. "I think we ought to concentrate on getting all these young people out of here."

"The poor lad's had the breath knocked out of him. That's all there is to it."

"He'd be up by now, you stupid man. You don't know what you're talking about."

"He's coming round!" Zoe was incredulous.

"Come on Barney," everybody started cheering.

"I still don't think—"

55

"Oh go and sit in the car, Joel."

Barney lifted his shoulder.

"Come on Barney, get back on your legs. You can do it!"

Everybody started cheering him on – even Toukie was shouting herself hoarse.

I wiped my face, my hand clutching Eric's arm, hope daring to rear its head.

"I love you, Barney!"

For one split second he looked straight at me and if I hadn't known better, I could have sworn he smiled. Then he stretched out a foreleg, grunted, heaved himself up, and stood trembling, dust-spattered and soaked in sweat.

"My goodness, that horse has got nine lives." Mrs Brayfield looked as if she'd seen a ghost.

"He's all right," I shrieked. "He can walk!"

Barney immediately butted me in the stomach and tried to drag me off towards Lace.

"I don't believe it." Zoe ran up, patting him like mad. "He's OK!" Everybody started yahooing and clapping and the Bevan brothers wolf-whistled just to show off. Barney shook himself like a dog and then yanked his head down to eat some grass.

"Get back on." Eric was so matter-of-fact I wondered if I'd heard him right. "Get back on, Alex, right now!"

"You've got to be joking." I turned round,

white-faced, still getting over the shock. Everybody fell silent.

Joel marched over to Barney, running his hand expertly down his foreleg, locating the blood to a two-inch scratch. "Are you out of your mind? Isn't it enough that the horse has walked away? You can't possibly expect the girl to ride."

"Be quiet, Joel."

"I beg your pardon?"

Eric completely ignored Joel and fixed me with a stony stare.

"Alexandra Johnson, don't argue. Just get back on. It's for your own good!"

I'd never heard him sound so serious.

"I-I can't." I could feel tears quivering in my eyes. There was no way I could get back on. I felt sick at the thought of it.

"You've not changed, have you? Mr High and Mighty." Joel suddenly let rip, his neck flushing, his hands clasping into fists. "I'd have thought after twenty years you'd have learnt something. But oh no, Eric Burgess just blasts through life, no regard for anyone's feelings. It's no wonder she left you for me. It was the best thing she ever did."

"Leave Tanya out of this." Eric was purple with rage. "You might have weaseled your way in there, O'Ryan, with your false charm, but you're not taking Alex. Why not admit it, the only reason you're here is to get back at me? I'm right aren't I?"

"Stop it!" I couldn't take it any longer. "You're both like kids. I can't believe you. I'm not some pawn in one of your silly games, I'm a human being."

"I'm warning you, Alex." Eric suddenly looked drained. "If you don't get back on I can't train you."

"I don't care." I'd really flipped now, oblivious to everybody watching. "I've had it with both of you, I don't need a trainer. I don't need anybody, I'll train myself."

"The vet's on his way." Jasper pushed through the huddled group of riders, his horse dripping with sweat, an urgent look in his eyes. He fell quiet when he saw Barney.

"You're too late," I snapped, well aware I was taking it out on him. "It's all over. The whole show has just gone kaput."

CHAPTER SIX

"He won't answer the door." Ash got out of the jeep in the stable yard and lifted Daisy from the back seat.

"The curtains are drawn and he told me to buzz off. He doesn't want Alex anywhere near the place."

Ash had just come back from Eric's cottage with the worst possible news.

"He's probably just saying that." Zoe screwed up her face, trying to look on the bright side.

"Eric always means what he says." I took Daisy's lead and coaxed her towards the common room. Ash followed with a dog blanket and Daisy's toy frog.

"The last time he went like this he didn't come out for three years." The concern on Ash's face stood out a mile.

Eric was an agoraphobic. After his accident he'd locked himself away and refused to take part in the world. If Barney hadn't bolted one day and dumped me in his garden I wouldn't have known he existed. We all thought he was cured. He'd started to live life again. Now he'd slipped right back.

"He wants you to look after Daisy, at least for the time being. God knows why. Perhaps so she can be near Barney." Ash stomped over to the fridge for a can of Coke. "He'll let me know when he wants her back. How's Barney? What did the vet say?"

Barney was at present in his stable feeling extremely sorry for himself but still managing to devour every titbit that came his way. When I sneaked back to his stable very quietly I kept catching him playing with Daisy's football.

"He's fine," I gulped, exhausted and deflated. "Just a little stiff, nothing to worry about."

Ash threw down his leather jacket and grabbed the mobile phone. "Better call the back man. You can never be too careful – old Brayfield says it was a bad fall. By the way, you look as if you've just walked through a hedge."

In eventing the horse always came first no matter what and the rider had to grit their teeth and shrug off pain like a dose of flu. At that moment my hip was on fire, I had bruises the size of saucers and I could quite happily have crumpled in a heap, preferably in Ash's arms. "Oh don't worry about me." I waved my hand dismissively and started frantically rearranging one of Zoe's flower displays. "I'm as fit as a fiddle." Ash was busy dialling another number, irritation cast in deep lines round his mouth.

I collapsed into a plastic chair and tried not to dissolve into tears. "It's no good," I said five minutes later. "I've got to see Eric!"

"Are you out of your mind?" Ash leapt up. "My parents will be with him now, and if he sees you he's likely to have another attack."

"I'm his friend," I yelled, the full force of rejection hitting me like a ton of bricks. "If it wasn't for me he wouldn't be like this."

"You've got a point there." His voice was ice cold.

I wanted to close my ears and bury my head in the sand. "You can't tell me what to do. I don't take orders from you."

"Well it's time you did." Ash leant towards me. "You nearly write off your horse, you agree to go on some stupid trip to Sweden. You suck up to Joel like a star-struck idiot. Not to mention being openly rude to my best livery owner and accusing me of being a two-timing rat. Just what are you planning next, Alex, because I'd really like to know."

"Stop it!" Zoe came back from the jeep, looking incredulous. "This is crazy. What's happened to the two lovebirds? What's happened to supporting each other through thick and thin? I used to think you guys had something really special but now look at you – you can't even be friends."

I gulped back a flood of tears and wanted the floor to open up. I was just having vague notions of waving an olive branch when Ruth Hanson pushed open the door behind Zoe flashing a megawatt smile and clutching hold of a bicycle chain.

"Oh Ashley darling," she said, completely ignoring me and Zoe. "Could you possibly help me with my bike?"

"Go ahead, darling." I scowled at Ash while inwardly trembling. "Help little Ruthie with her chain."

I dragged Daisy, still scoffing a mouthful of food towards the door, wanting to escape to Timbuctoo. "Oh and by the way." I flicked my head back towards Ash. "We're finished!"

"Don't you think you were a little rash?" Camilla was sprawled on the grass holding The Hawk on an extended lead rope listening to the whole gory story. "Whatever happened to fighting for your man?"

Zoe was lying on her stomach scouring the horoscope column for rays of hope. "It says here under Scorpio that you should focus all your attention on what really matters."

"Exactly." I adjusted the dark sunglasses which were hiding my bloodshot eyes and reached for the suntan lotion. "From now on all my attentions are going to be focused on Barney. He's the only man in my life."

"Of course you seriously need your head examining." Cam went across to The Hawk who was about to devour someone's coat.

Cam always had a string of at least five boys in tow and thought anybody who was single had either a personality problem or BO. "I thought Ruth was OK," she said. "She kind of grows on you."

"Yes," I answered, pulling a daisy to pieces. "Like a wart. Now can we please stop talking about Ash? I don't love him, I never have loved him and I never will love him."

"Yes, Alex. Whatever you say, dear."

"You can't put it off for ever." Zoe was almost violently shaking me.

I hadn't slept all night and I was avoiding Joel like the plague. I'd trudged up to Eric's cottage at lunchtime and yelled through the letterbox but he'd shoved a note back saying he was perfectly all right and he didn't need me sticking my beak in, and adding, "P.S. Could you please tell Ash to fetch me some sprouts and could you make sure Daisy has her wormer."

I sent him a note back saying I thought he was a wimp. Then I felt guilty and sent him another note apologizing for asking about Tanya. I didn't realize about Joel. I said I'd been a fool and could he possibly forgive me. I waited half an hour and all I heard was the television turned up full blast.

"Planet Earth to Alex, is there anybody there?" Zoe wrinkled her nose and then suddenly looked serious. "You've got to tell him, Alex," she urged, "before it's too late."

Joel O'Ryan was sitting in the caravan-cum-office writing extensive notes. I saw him through the dust-caked window and felt like the lion in *The Wizard of Oz*. "Get a grip of yourself, girl," I muttered. I took a massive deep breath. After all, what was the very worst he could do?

"Enter!"

Joel raised his head allowing me a thin smile and very deliberately laid down his pen. "So, you've finally arrived."

"I'm sorry," I mumbled, throwing back my shoulders and trying to look authoritative. "But I've changed my mind, I don't want to go to Sweden."

"I see." He pushed back his chair.

"It's not that I don't appreciate the offer but I don't think I'm ready. Barney's not ready. It's too soon."

"I agree."

"Oh." I was temporarily thrown. I didn't

expect it to be this easy. The palms of my hands suddenly broke out in a clammy sweat.

Joel smiled sweetly. "I was deceived in the beginning because you were Eric's protégée. He's always had a good eye for talent. But there's no easy way to say this except you haven't got what it takes. I'm sorry to have built up your hopes but you'll never get to the top. I hope you respect me for being honest."

"Oh." I crumbled, blinding tears building up at the back of my eyes. I was determined not to break down. My bottom lip was quivering but I forcibly held myself together.

"It's a tough old world." Joel treated me to another of his sugar-coated smiles. "I'm sure you'll make it as an instructor, or a stable manager. Have you ever thought of being a vet's nurse?"

I collapsed in the tack room an hour later wondering how people coped with total and utter rejection. I'd been wandering round like a lost soul and I still couldn't come to terms with it. I was a failure, an also-ran.

"Crikey, what's happened?" Zoe rushed in, her hair spiked up on end, a dirty smudge under one eye. "I've been waiting for you for ages."

I told her in crucifying detail exactly how Joel had stripped me of every scrap of confidence.

"The pig!" she retorted, outraged and instantly protective. "Where does he get off?"

"It's true though, Zoe. It's my fault Barney fell at that log pile. I got the striding completely wrong – I could have killed him."

"You should never have been jumping it in the first place," she snorted. "It's like asking an inexperienced actor to play Shakespeare in the West End, it's ridiculous."

I knew she was trying to help but it didn't make me feel the slightest bit better. She'd brought Daisy in with her, who now sat looking up at me with huge sad eyes, unable to work out what was wrong.

"You're not going to let this man beat you," Zoe harrumphed. "You and Barney have come too far. Eric believed in you. You've got to believe in yourself."

"I can't," I wailed. "I've had enough, I can't take any more."

"Huh. If Eric heard you talking like that he'd have another attack. Remember his keyword, persistence, persistence."

"You don't understand." I jumped up in despair, hardly able to focus. Barney's saddle was hung neatly on one of the racks, well oiled and gleaming. A painful reminder.

I let my fingers trail down the saddle flap and turned to Zoe. "Eric was right," I gulped. "I should have got back on. It was the biggest mistake I've ever made. You see . . ." I looked at her with eyes as lost and frightened as Daisy. "I've lost my nerve."

"You're not going to hide away!" Zoe fished out the hair crimpers from the bottom of her wardrobe and went to work.

Depression swamped me like a blanket but for Zoe's sake I'd have to go through with it. She was more than just a brick, she was a lifeline.

Joel was holding a slide show that night in the Dutch barn and Eric was supposed to be giving a talk on fitness training but nobody really expected him to turn up. Ash was sure to be there, and all the Pony Club members.

"I can't go through with it," I whimpered. "I'll be a laughing stock."

Zoe got out some eyelash curlers. She was convinced a complete make-over was just what was called for to pep up my spirits.

I flinched. "I'm sorry, Zoe." I sounded so pitiful. "But it's going to take more than bubble bath and hair crimpers to sort out my life."

The slide show was well underway as I hobbled up the drive in Zoe's two-inch heels. I'd bought Daisy a new lead especially for the occasion and some of the old "knock 'em dead" spirit was filtering through my veins. How dare Joel write me off as a rider? What did he know anyway? And where was Zoe? She'd said she'd be here by now.

I yanked down the short skirt feeling as leggy as a gazelle and opened the arched door. It was dark inside and Joel was already underway pointing to a picture of the showjumper Guy Goosen. "Now can anybody tell me how to stride out a double combination?"

I slid into a chair next to a boy so broad-shouldered he made Superman look like a choirboy. He smiled a toothy grin and I felt instantly protected. Daisy snuffled under the chair legs and sighed deeply.

A warm solid core of pride was starting to well up inside me. Zoe was right: "If you can't beat 'em, join 'em." I stroked my stockinged knees and glanced around for Ash. It was so dark I had to squint and a blob of mascara glued up my right eye.

"And of course here we have Mark Todd, probably the greatest rider in the world." Joel didn't let up for a minute.

"Is he married?" Spanner, the girl at Jasper's party, yelled out.

The boy next to me offered me a packet of cheese straws and fixed his eyes on my newly plucked eyebrows which looked as if they'd been worried by a terrier.

"Now can anybody tell me what is meant by a

hog's back?" Joel was scouring the aisles. I slid down in the chair and heard the door click open behind me.

I was just beginning to think that if Joel was going to ask questions I was going to make a fast exit. Then the boy next to me leaned over really close, grabbed my hand, and whispered, "Do you believe in love at first sight?"

I leapt up, panic-stricken, before I realized what I was doing. The chair screeched back, nearly tilting over, and I collided into the arms of someone who felt vaguely familiar.

"Alex!" Ash was glaring down at me, his blond hair scraped back off his forehead with hair gel making him look extra-stern. "What are you doing here? And what are you wearing? You look terrible."

I was just about to mumble an answer, not wanting to let go of him, when someone flicked on a light switch and I saw Ruth standing next to him.

"Oh," I croaked. "Hello." My senses were reeling. She looked so gorgeous, so simple in jeans and a striped shirt. I had a vision of a ship being wrecked against hard rocks.

I didn't see Daisy lope for the open door. All I could think of was Ash and Ruth. Ruth and Ash. A couple.

The screeching tyres drowned out all noise, all reason. I heard the yelp, the thud, the voices.

"Daisy!" I ran towards the door in slow motion, in my own private nightmare, knowing instinctively what had happened.

Zoe's dad was crouched by the front tyres of the Land Rover Discovery, his shoulders slumped. Zoe was standing, a hand over her mouth.

Ash came up behind me, taking in the scene, running to help.

"It was an accident." Mr Jackson stood up, guilt-stricken and shocked. "She just ran straight out . . ."

CHAPTER SEVEN

"She was trying to get to Eric," I gulped, trembling from head to foot. "Please, Mr Jackson, can't we go any faster?"

The Land Rover swung round a double bend and Daisy struggled and then lay back gasping, her usually bloodshot eyes drained white. "It's all right, darling, not long now. Don't be scared."

I loosened the blanket we'd wrapped round her and pushed her long ears back off her pretty face.

"She's a tough cookie," Mr Jackson smiled. "She'll pull through."

Ash had stayed behind to pick up Eric and let the vet know we were on our way. The lights were on at the surgery as we pulled into the car park.

"I'll carry her." Mr Jackson tenderly picked her up in both arms, while I ran to hold open the door. "There's a good girl, sssh now."

One of the veterinary nurses came across straight away and started to take details. Age, sex, name, previous medical history.

The answers rolled off my tongue but I couldn't even remember saying anything.

Jack Douglas strode out of an examination room looking confident and reassuring. "I came in as soon as I could," he said, recognition filtering into his eyes. "Let's get the old girl onto the table."

In the last ten minutes Daisy's condition had deteriorated. Her lovely soft brown eyes had closed heavily; the red eyelashes were highlighted under the special spotlight. Her tail was clamped tightly between her legs, her back bent.

The vet set to work immediately, listening to her heart, feeling her body. I knew it wasn't good. He reached for a needle. I knew I'd never forgive myself. The new lead was still in my hand, useless.

"We've got to operate." Jack Douglas was tight lipped and strained. "Is there anyone who can sign a consent form?"

"She's ruptured her spleen." The veterinary nurse guided me to a chair where I sat and stared into space.

"Eric should be here any minute," I mumbled. "I d-don't know what to do."

"Has Daisy had anything to eat?" The nurse had to do her job.

"I don't know, no, n-not since lunchtime," I remembered.

"Listen love, do you want a cup of tea? You're as white as a ghost."

"It's all my fault," I sobbed, my chest rising

and falling. "I'm so hopeless, this should never have happened. If she dies . . ."

The door suddenly swung on its hinges and Eric appeared with Ash guiding the wheelchair. I'd never seen anybody's face look so bereft. It was as if all the life had been switched off – he was gaunt and grey and frightened – and it was all my fault.

"Where is she?" he growled, staring straight at the nurse.

"If you could just sign here." She held out a sheet of paper.

"I want to see my dog."

Jack Douglas appeared in a green gown and a pair of thin plastic gloves. "It's all right, Kate. Eric, if you'd like to come this way."

Mr Jackson went across to the reception desk clutching the blanket and looking drained.

"I think I'd better take you home." He turned to me, trying to smile. "They'll let us know how the operation goes."

"But I can't just leave," I choked. "What about Daisy? What about Eric?"

"I think it's a good idea." Ash's face was unreadable.

Is that what we had come to, two strangers staring at each other across an empty room?

"You'd better take her lead." I was going to go to pieces at any moment. "You will ring, won't you?"

It didn't sound like my voice at all. It sounded like a lost frightened child. For a second a flood of warmth flickered in Ash's eyes and then the shutters came down and we were a hundred miles apart.

"You'll be the first to know."

When I got home, there were reminders of Daisy everywhere: dog bowls, chewed bones, a plastic hoop. My parents were devastated when they heard and plied me with cups of hot chocolate.

The phone call came through at 2.30 in the morning.

"She's OK." Ash sounded exhausted. "She's pulled round from the anaesthetic. Jack said we can take her home."

I had to sit down with relief.

"Of course, she's not out of the woods yet. Alex, are you there?"

I pulled myself together and mumbled an affirmative.

"There could be complications."

Every single curtain was drawn as I approached the cottage. It was a brilliant hot day and almost too bright and colourful for decency. It wasn't a day for unhappiness.

The front door swung open.

"Eric?"

He was over by the fireplace.

"Ssssh." He put his finger to his lips and pointed to the sofa. "She's asleep."

I could tell by his face that it wasn't good. He looked as if he was going through his own private hell.

Daisy was laid out on the flowered cushions, her lovely soft face drawn and pinched. Her coat had been shaved where she'd had the operation.

"She's given up." Eric was inconsolable. "She's lost all interest. She's just lying there and waiting for death."

I felt as if someone had slapped me across the face with reality.

"No," I mumbled. "She's going to get better, she's got to."

She half lifted her head when she saw me and then fell back, her eyes smiling recognition, but dull, white, listless.

"Oh darling, you poor little lamb. What have I done to you?" The pain in my chest was almost suffocating.

"I'm so sorry." I turned to Eric. "You must really hate me."

He had a hand over his eyes, fighting back emotion, trying to keep back the glaring agonizing pain of possibly losing his best friend.

"It was my fault," his voice grated and broke off. "If I hadn't been feeling so sorry for myself . . .

75

I shouldn't have left her with you. The poor girl just wanted to come home. I caused it."

"No, no, you're wrong, listen to me. It was an accident." I had to convince him. I couldn't stand to see him torturing himself.

Suddenly an idea started to form inside my head, like a bolt out of the blue.

"I've got to go!" I leapt up. Frantic.

Eric jerked his head towards me.

"I'll be back as soon as I can." I kissed the top of Daisy's head and made for the door, hope rising like boiling milk. "Just one thing, when you hear me come back, will you open the window?"

There was no time to lose. I rushed back to the stables. I burst through the tack room door, and saw Barney's saddle and bridle. But I reached for his head collar.

He was standing at the back of his stable, resting a leg and looking bored out of his mind. "Come on boy, we're going on a journey."

Without any encouragement he thrust his nose into the head collar and barged towards the door.

He was skitting sideways as we cut across the parkland and made for the wood. I was dodging flying hoofs and desperately trying to keep control, wishing I'd put on his bridle instead. Everybody knew it was easier to ride a horse than lead one. Especially when that horse was a super-fit, part-bred Arab like Barney. And heading for his favourite place.

By the time we reached the cottage my right arm felt as if it was jolted out of its socket. Barney kept glaring at me with disdain as if wanting to know why I wasn't riding.

The sitting room window swept open and Barney let out a volley of bucks and squealed in delight. But instead of looking at the window his eyes were peeled on the back door where Daisy usually came rushing out. This time she didn't. I gulped back a lump of emotion. How on earth did you tell a horse that his best friend was hovering between life and death?

Barney and Daisy had been drawn together right from the very beginning – when Barney had been a renegade and did everything wrong. Daisy would sit by the edge of the dressage arena and bark encouragement. They would share an ice cream and follow each other round the paddock. I'd even taught Daisy to lead Barney by his lead rope. They were inseparable friends.

Now Daisy needed someone to give her the will to live. And that person had to be Barney.

"What are you doing?" Eric was stunned.

Opening both sides of the window I let Barney thrust his head through.

Daisy was already propped up on her

shoulder, her tail bobbing up and down. She was ecstatic.

"Quick." I let go of Barney and ran inside, intent on pushing the sofa up by the window.

Eric was in a daze and no help whatsoever.

"It's all right, Daisy. Barney's not going anywhere. Let's just get you over here."

Barney plunged his head back through the window, trailing a whole branch of a shrub. It was only when he reached down to sniff at Daisy that he realized something was wrong. The concern flooded into his eyes until they turned almost black. He was quivering all over. Very tenderly he examined Daisy's stitches, whickering and snorting and looking at me in panic.

"It's all right, boy, she's going to be fine."

Daisy started licking his nose and gave a deep throaty howl.

"I don't believe it." Eric's mouth quivered with relief, tears starting to streak down his cheeks.

"That's what people need when they're in hospital," I babbled on. "Something to bring them round, jerk them out of it. Anything was worth a try. I figured we had nothing to lose."

Eric nodded understanding, pulling himself together, finding his old strength. "Well, Alex, you little diamond, I think you've just saved the old girl's life!"

CHAPTER EIGHT

Daisy was going to be all right. Jack Douglas made a house visit in the afternoon and announced she was out of danger. There was no further internal damage.

I took Barney back to the stables and decided to lunge him on the arena. Zoe said she'd have to watch because last time I got the lunge rein wrapped round my waist and Barney came to a grinding halt. It was really difficult to do but the secret was to fix your eye contact on the horse's shoulder and that way you didn't go dizzy. Lunging was really good for suppling the muscles and general obedience.

Barney stamped across the loose sand, furious that I wasn't riding and determined to be a menace.

Zoe plonked herself down by the railings and fed the ducks the remains of her cold pizza.

Barney started circling me on the end of the long rein, bucking and prancing, weaving in, and showing off. I dug in my heel and tried not to move about.

"Flick the whip at him." Zoe tried to be

helpful but every time I moved the lunge whip Barney shot forward.

"He's just testing you," Zoe shouted, deciding to give Reggie a bath with a wet sponge.

I asked Barney to canter and surprisingly he obliged. Stray thoughts of Sweden and super-stardom drifted into my mind on a black cloud. How could I have been so stupid? Thank goodness I hadn't got round to telling my parents about the plan.

"Of course all the top riders lunge their horses," continued Zoe just as Barney came to a thumping great halt and refused to move forward.

Red in the face and hot and bothered I decided to call it a day. Zoe was just about to tell me for the hundredth time how she'd accidentally set fire to the school domestic science kitchens when Ruth rattled up on her mountain bike looking radiant all in white with her hair slicked back with gel.

"I thought you were always supposed to finish on a good note?" she asked. "Not let them get away with things?" She flashed me a pearly white smile and first degree murder became a distinct possibility.

"I've just come to see Sunny. She's such a poppet and Ash rides her so beautifully."

I tried not to gnash my teeth and surrep-titiously wiped a droplet of sweat from my top lip.

Ruth looked as if she never perspired. She probably didn't know what it was to have sticky palms or smelly feet.

Very craftily and purposefully she drew me to one side and pretended to take an interest in Barney.

"Look," she whispered. "I really hope there's no hard feelings. Ash said you two had split up. I'd hate you to think I'm a man rustler, treading on toes and all that."

"No, no," I squeaked, feeling as if a steam-roller was running over both my feet.

"Oh that's all right then." She faked relief. "He said you were just a stop-gap, it wasn't anything serious. I wonder . . ." She hesitated, giving me just enough time to recover before she gave me another blast. "We're thinking about jetting off to Paris for my birthday. I know it's a funny thing to ask but I wondered if you could tell me his favourite colour?"

"So what's Mary Poppins said this time?" Zoe twitched her nose and pulled one of her curls, which always meant she was being protective.

"Oh nothing," I gulped, leaning up against Barney's shoulder to steady my quaking knees. If only I could surround my heart with a sheet of reinforced steel. Was this it? Would I have to carry a broken heart around for the rest of my life?

"Well, whatever it was," Zoe pursed her lips and scuffed one of her Doc Marten boots, "she was lying. I've had a book out of the library for three weeks on body language and as sure as I'm a redhead she was touching her nose every other second. That girl tells more porky pies than all the political parties put together."

Camilla thundered into the common room half an hour later, blonde hair fanning out, blue eyes flashing.

Her mother pulled up outside the stables with the Range Rover and trailer and The Hawk sounding as if he was about to crash through the ramp.

"He's really done it this time." Cam collapsed in a heap, fanning herself with a newspaper and dramatically putting a hand on her forehead. "I think the man's gone mad. Either that or he's trying to make the Sutton Vale extinct by killing off all the members."

"Cam, will you calm down for thirty seconds and speak in an intelligible form?" Zoe handed her a bottle of lemonade which fizzed up all over her leather boots.

"It's Jolly Joel." Cam momentarily stopped screeching. "He's decided on the spur of the moment to have a cross-country competition tomorrow and he's been putting us over fences as big as Becher's Brook. The Hawk's gone lame and

Mummy's threatening to sue. Toukie says she can't sleep at night. There's mutiny at the camp, mark my words."

Cam took a huge deep breath and announced that Zoe had five penalties for skipping the practice and Joel wanted her to go first in the cross-country tomorrow.

"He can go and whistle," Zoe snorted. "There's no way I'm taking Lace round one of his kamikaze courses."

A little idea pinged in my brain and wouldn't go away. "Oh, I don't know. It might be possible. And it would wipe that smug smile off his face."

"Forget it, Alex. I'd rather do deep-sea diving. Unless . . ."

Suddenly a strangled shriek escaped from the stable yard and The Hawk hobbled past intent on reaching the feed room.

"Camilla, don't you think you ought to take your feet off the table and go and help your poor mother?"

I couldn't carry on like this. I had to get back in the saddle. And the cross-country competition was the perfect motivation.

I told my parents I was staying at Zoe's and hung around in Barney's stable until everybody had gone home. The yard was deserted. The only noise was the steady munching of hay and Reggie and Nigel flapping their wings and splashing around in a cat tray they used as a water bath.

I came out of the stable towards the feed room with my heart banging like jungle drums. How can anybody lose their nerve to this extent? All I could think about was crashing to the ground and Barney thrashing his legs in blind panic, unable to get up.

Mentally blanking my mind I picked up the saddle and bridle and went back to the stable. As soon as Barney felt the girth tighten he started trembling with excitement. "Come on boy." I fastened my riding hat and opened the door. "Let's try to find some of the old magic."

It was perfectly simple. All I had to do was put my foot in the stirrup and swing into the saddle. Barney stood obediently bending his neck and trying to make it as easy as possible. They say horses have a sixth sense and I think he knew I was petrified.

I'd done this a million times before, it was no big deal. I turned the stirrup the right way and gathered the reins in my left hand. I lifted up my left foot and prepared to hop round and spring up. But the sick feeling hit me in the stomach like cramp and I bottled out in a pathetic heap. I stood trembling, leaning against the saddle, wondering what on earth to do next.

84

I was finished. I was a complete waste of space and I didn't deserve a horse like Barney.

It was a clear night, just starting to go dark, the moon a pale milky glow. Pent-up tears of frustration slid slowly down my cheeks as I wrapped my arms round Barney's neck and tried to say sorry. Joel had been right all along. I just wasn't cut out to be a top rider. I didn't have what it took – that extra drive and determination, that extra special something.

Suddenly the overhead lights burst into a yellow glow. I shot my head round; just me and Barney standing in the middle of the sand arena. I felt like a bewildered rabbit caught in the glare of a headlight.

"You could be good if you stuck at it," the voice bellowed across from the gate; rich, confident with an undercurrent of emotion.

I turned round, my knees trembling but this time with relief. I grinned until my face felt as if it would split in two. "Of course I'd need a good trainer!"

"The best," Eric shouted back. "And of course they're not easy to find." He was pushing his chair back and forth, enjoying the banter, remembering old times. "But I suppose you could always make do with me."

I flung down Barney's reins and raced across the arena, leaping over the gate and throwing my arms around Eric's neck. "I'm so sorry," I cried. "I've been such a fool."

"All right, all right, you silly mare, enough of the amateur dramatics." He rubbed the top of my head like a dog and straightened his tie and jacket. "Now, unless I'm very much mistaken, we've got our work cut out. In case you've forgotten, competition rules state you have to be in the saddle, not dribbling along on foot. Now, go and get mounted up before I lose my patience and call you a simpering ninny."

We trained on and on. First a pole on the ground. Then a nine-inch jump. Every time I started to bottle out Eric went right back to the beginning. The stable clock chimed midnight by the time we reached two foot.

"You see this is where Joel goes wrong." Eric was animated. "There's no need for all this galloping and jumping high fences. You've got to get the foundations right. Build up the confidence. Push too hard and it's like building a castle on sand – it'll disentegrate before your very eyes."

Barney popped over a parallel, happy and relaxed, snapping up his forelegs in a balanced style.

"Let your hands move forward," Eric encouraged. "Follow the movement, flow with the horse over the jump."

I was enjoying myself, I was up in the saddle

and placing Barney at jumps with an accurate eye. How could I ever have been so stupid as to listen to Joel? Eric was the best trainer in the world.

By one o'clock I'd got back my nerve and my confidence. I was ready to take on Joel and make him eat his words. I dismounted, breathless and pumping with adrenalin, feeling on top of the world.

"Remember," Eric said, "the future isn't a gift, it's an achievement. You get out what you put in. You've got to be persistent."

Barney butted me in the shoulder as we walked back to the stables.

"His courses are always windy." Eric started discussing tactics. "He'll throw in a bogus fence when you least expect it. There'll be wide open spaces, then the tightest turns. You've got to be on your mettle. He won't make it easy."

I was listening to every word.

"We'll go through it all again tomorrow."

"Today," I corrected. "You will be there, won't you? I can't do it without you."

Eric's face momentarily darkened, his eyes shadowed with doubt.

"Eric?"

"You don't know what you're asking, Alex. It's too much." He glanced down at his legs with a look of self-loathing.

"If I can face him, you can." I turned round,

pulling Barney to a sharp halt. "You can't run away for ever, you can't hide away from the past."

The words shot out before I realized. Then I remembered his stress attack and guilt tore into me. "I'm sorry, I didn't mean to say that."

"But you're right, aren't you?" Bitterness subsided to show vulnerability and fear.

"I'm just a scared old man. I lecture you about guts and courage but I can't even face up to a scallywag like O'Ryan."

"I never said that," I backtracked, desperately not wanting to upset him.

"Tanya O'Neil was my fiancée," Eric started, pain etched over his face. "She was the most beautiful girl I'd ever known. I loved her. I thought she loved me. Then I was offered a job in America for a year. When I came home O'Ryan had stepped into my shoes. We'd been best friends since junior school. He'd taken my girl."

"And you've never spoken since?" I could hardly believe it.

"I got the job as *chef d'équipe* of the Olympic team and O'Ryan never forgave me. I reported him, you see, for cruelty to horses. It was all a very long time ago."

"Wow." I was completely shellshocked.

"I've come back out of the woodwork now." Eric visibly stiffened. "Joel heard about you and Barney and thought he'd knock me down a peg or two. He was out to destroy you, Alex. You didn't stand a chance."

"I just wish you'd told me all this in the beginning."

"Old wounds don't heal easily." Eric allowed himself a thin smile. "Nobody likes raking up the past."

"So what are you going to do now?" I twiddled with Barney's reins, still awestruck.

"I'm going to go home, have a shave, find a clean shirt and tie, and face Joel man to man." Eric pushed his wheelchair forward, his features lightening. "I think we've both got something to prove, don't you?"

CHAPTER NINE

The cross-country course was a hive of activity: huddled groups of riders trudging around from fence to fence, sweating, stamping horses flying in all directions, worried parents pacing around.

"This is going to be a nightmare." Zoe put on her Mafia-style dark sunglasses and nearly walked straight into a hairy cob.

Toukie bulldozed towards us wearing a back protector back to front and resembling a deformed turtle. "Jasper's locked himself in the portable loo and refuses to come out," she screeched. "I never thought he'd be such a wimp."

Mrs Brayfield marched up swinging a jumping whip and having overheard the conversation said she'd give him a good talking-to. "It's just like Jasper to hog the public amenity – no thought for anybody else."

Toukie went on to tell us how last night she'd put a marmalade scrub on her feet thinking it might be relaxing but now her feet just felt gritty.

"You silly fool," Zoe snorted. "You're supposed to wash it off!"

Barney was standing in the horsebox as cool

as a cucumber, gently pulling at a hay net, looking like a racehorse in his best show rug and bandages.

I was overcome by a fresh wave of anxiety. I was frantically tussling with my memory, trying to recall the exact route from the coffin to the railway sleepers. Joel's course was as big as Sherwood Forest and everybody was freaking out.

Camilla suddenly appeared in denim overalls and her hair scrunched up in a bun carrying a grooming kit and wearing yellow marigolds. Zoe gaped and I felt my knees shaking.

"So where's the equine personality of the year?" she grinned, pulling out a dandy brush.

As Cam didn't know a mane comb from a hoof pick it was a really sweet gesture. "Anything to wipe the smile off Jolly Joel's face," she scowled, picking at a perfectly manicured tangerine-painted nail. "And where's Eric?"

I knew he wouldn't be early. There was still an hour to go before I was due to ride. Everybody was warming up, trying to summon up courage, wondering what on earth we were all doing.

"Gunfight at the Sutton Vale." Zoe shot into the horsebox and brought out the saddle and bridle. "Shake a leg, Alex. It's time to get ready."

As I rode into the collecting ring Joel's face was rigid with tension. I pushed Barney onto a long stride, sitting deep in the saddle. Joel was perched on a shooting stick, ordering everybody about, trying not to notice the sudden silence as Barney took centre stage.

Barney marched forward, supercharged. My confidence rallied and grew until I felt we could jump the moon. I was sitting on top of a Ferrari and Joel knew it. No wonder he was puckering his lips with agitation. I was going to do this for Eric, for times past. Nothing was going to stand in our way – we were going to go clear.

Barney's lopey ears swished back and forth. Zoe came rushing across, pointing at her watch, looking desperate. "Quarter to eleven, where is he?"

A sudden long low howl made my eyes sting with tears. Daisy! Barney let out a chorus of high bucks and we turned 180 degrees to see a dark green Rolls Royce purring up to the collecting ring with a uniformed chauffeur at the wheel and Eric in the back seat.

"What on earth?" Camilla came bouncing up, eyes on stalks, with a lead rope round her neck. "What's Eric up to now?"

"This is style," Jasper trundled across, looking peaky, keen to be in on the gossip. "Where did he get that, out of a Christmas cracker?"

Barney immediately broke into a trot and trembling with excitement squeezed his nose into the half wound-down window, jabbing his bit on the tinted glass. Daisy was lying on the back seat, sprawled out, with a tartan rug over her, looking like royalty.

"She's fighting fit," Eric grinned, his eyes crinkling. "And will you kindly control your horse – he's slobbering all down my best jacket."

Joel looked as sour as gone-off milk. "Well, Burgess, you've certainly pushed the boat out this time."

Eric moved smoothly from the Rolls Royce to his chair looking as sprightly as a new pin and knowing it. His cravat was so starchy white it could stand up by itself.

I was exploding with pride.

"I'm going to prove to you that this horse is the best in the country." Eric eyed Joel like a heavyweight boxer.

"Just like old times," said Joel with an under-current of sarcasm.

"May the best man win." Eric offered his hand for a formal handshake.

"You're on." Joel at least managed to rise to the occasion.

Barney snorted and stamped the ground and I knew we had our work cut out. I couldn't let Eric down.

"Well, Alex." Joel looked at his watch and then at me. "I think it's time you started warming up, don't you?"

*

The ground just disappeared beneath us. Barney was on top form, devouring the practice fences, turning, jumping, pulling up on a sixpence.

"Way to go!" Camilla got completely carried away from the ringside and was behaving more in keeping with a football match.

Zoe ran forward and tightened Barney's brushing boots and Eric insisted on one of the fences being lowered. Joel could hardly believe it and was almost tutting under his breath. Eric shot him a quelling glance and ordered me to take it from three strides out. "Good rhythm, keep him straight."

I pulled down my cross-country shirt and turned in a ten-metre circle. I didn't quite fix my eye on the jump.

The crowd suddenly parted with the sunshine behind to highlight Ash and Ruth sauntering along arm in arm. My heart lurched and before I knew it Barney had ducked down his head, charged at the fence and knocked off the top rail.

Eric was mortified. Ruth almost ran forward feigning concern, asking if I was using too much leg.

"Why don't you keep your legs to yourself?" I wanted to snap back, but instead buried my head in my chin guard and felt the colour scorch into my cheeks.

"Try to be a rider rather than a passenger,"

said Eric at his sarcastic best. Joel was loving every minute.

I saw Ash a few feet away mouthing good luck but when our eyes locked mine slithered away. I couldn't think about him right now – I couldn't be distracted.

"Three – two – one." Joel pressed a stop-watch and brought down his arm. "*Go!*"

We bounded forward. Instantly I knew we were as one, that remarkable exhilarating feeling of horse and rider in perfect harmony.

I eased the reins, he lengthened his stride and we soared over the straw bales. Next the log pile, then the wall. It was all so easy – we were the perfect team.

The ground dipped downhill and the fences became bigger. I was riding like a demon now, crouched low, hands and legs working together, thundering into the jumps without a single check.

Toukie's pink and white cross-country shirt flitted in the woods ahead. She was still on the course. I checked my stopwatch – one minute, forty-five seconds. What on earth was she doing?

Barney grabbed his bit and hurled me over a three-foot hedge giving it yards of daylight. I'd never ridden him this fast – he was starting to take a hold.

"Steady boy, steady, you're going too fast."

We flew over a post and rail.

A whistle screeched and I turned a blind bend. Barney slipped, struggled and regained his balance; woodchips were flying in all directions. Suddenly somebody loomed up ahead, waving us down, frantically trying to bring us to a halt.

But it was too late. Barney was out of control. I couldn't stop.

"Hold him!" someone shouted from the ropes. "Turn his head!"

I yanked on the reins but Barney was rigid with power and adrenalin. We had to go forward.

It soon became clear what the problem was. Toukie had jumped into the alternative which was a small bounce and Candy wouldn't jump out. They were stuck. The only other option was the huge corner which Eric had warned me not to jump.

Barney seemed to have made up his mind. This was crazy – the word kamikaze echoed in my head like a death-knell.

"Barney – no!"

The slightest error of judgement could mean a fall. I tried to think, tried to function – not too close to the edge nor too deep in which case the spread may be too wide. Keep him between hand and leg – hold a line!

A huge clod of soil flew up into my eye, pelting me full on so I was completely blinded. All I could feel were Barney's shoulders coming upwards, stretching, heaving, reaching for the back rail.

"Please God, keep us safe!"

I clung to a handful of mane and imagined somersaulting. My back protector dug reassuringly into my chest. I could feel a sudden rush of air on my cheeks – then the descent. We were clear. Barney rocked slightly, staggered forward, tossing me back into the saddle, and stormed on.

A huge wave of applause went up from everyone watching. I was still frozen to the saddle, my eye was streaming buckets and I had a lopsided view of everything around me.

Somehow I managed to steer Barney up the hill and kick on just when it was needed. I couldn't see my stopwatch. I couldn't see anything. I was in the hands of the gods.

Barney jumped the last two fences by himself, clearing the last at an angle. On the run-in to the finish line he seemed to gather speed rather than run out of steam. We flew over the finish, straight through a string and into the car park where I nearly collided into somebody's car and then got my reins tied up round an aerial.

Barney sauntered back to the others like the cat who'd got the cream while I quivered and gasped and wondered if I'd ever recover.

Zoe ran forward looking awe-struck, clipping

on a lead rein and leading me in like a Grand National winner.

"You did it!" Cam was going dotty. "You've knocked a whole minute off the best time of the day." She was patting Barney's neck as if it was going out of fashion.

"Even Mark Todd couldn't have jumped that corner any better." Zoe opened a packet of mints for Barney and scoffed three herself. "You're a star, Alex. Everybody's saying so."

There was no sign of Eric. I slithered out of the saddle, rucking up the stirrups and loosening the girth and surcingle. It was important for cross-country to always have an over-girth for extra safety. My hands were trembling so much I couldn't peel off my gloves.

"Here." Cam passed me a folded piece of paper. "Eric left this. He wanted you to have it straight away."

"Where is he?" I unfolded it clumsily, trying to avoid Barney butting me in the back. There were just two words, scribbled in scrawly capital letters but saying more than a thousand words. "PEAK PERFORMANCE." I hadn't let him down.

"You always were a cantankerous old so-and-so." Joel O'Ryan's petulant voice filtered over from the caravan.

"Oh belt up, you sour-faced mothball, and for

once in your life admit defeat." Eric was loving every minute.

"I told you there'd be a showdown," Zoe winked and we all fell quiet.

"You haven't heard the last of this." Joel turned on his heel, his face pale. "She's not that good."

"Oh buzz off before you make yourself look a right nelly. I'll see you at the championships – that's if you can stand the pace."

Joel gaped and then flounced off, his shoulders sagging.

Barney rested his head on my shoulder and pulled a goofy expression. I'd been a fool and a star-struck idiot but I'd won back Eric and my confidence. I'd never be so stupid again.

"Alex?" The voice was unmistakeable.

I felt the hairs on the back of my neck prickle to attention and an electric current run up my spine.

"What do you want?" I couldn't believe I was being so rude. A few days ago Ash Burgess had been the love of my life.

"I'm proud of you. I just want to say you rode brilliantly – I couldn't have done better myself. Is that OK, do I have permission to talk to you?"

Just gazing into his cornflower-blue eyes made me tremble like a greyhound. I was melting to butter at the speed of light when suddenly Ruth shoved past Camilla and latched on to his arm nearly cutting off the blood supply. Her smile said it all – hands off or else.

"Well, I'm not proud of you," I rallied, trying to keep my bottom lip from quivering. "And I couldn't give two hoots whether you watch me ride or not."

Ruth gasped and Eric burst out laughing. Infuriated I spun round and smacked my head right into Barney's. "And you shouldn't be earwigging either," I snapped, dragging him off for some grass.

CHAPTER TEN

"I can't face it!" I collapsed in a heap on Zoe's bedroom floor staring up at a poster of an Anglo-Arab galloping on the beach and wishing I could be as free as the wind.

"Nonsense," Zoe pouted. "Now listen to Auntie Zoe. There's no such word as 'can't'. What you need is a good dose of confidence and I know just how . . ."

"Oh no, please, not another make-over!" I cowered pathetically as if she was brandishing red-hot irons.

It was the evening of the Sutton Vale disco and cross-country presentation and as overall winner I had to be there.

"Can't somebody stand in for me like they do with the big stars?" I squeaked. "Pretend I'm in Hollywood or something, Hollyhead would do, anything, but don't make me go tonight."

I knew I sounded simpering but I didn't care. "My heart can't stand it, I shall crack up and die."

"Oh poppycock, there's plenty more fish in the sea. Now get a grip." Zoe reached for the hair rollers.

I covered my head with a magazine and she gave me one of her beady-eyed stares. "Do you want my help or not?"

When we were ready, Zoe had to drag me to the disco. It was being held in the barn where the slide show had taken place and was meant to be an end-of-week celebration. Most people were celebrating the fact that they were still alive.

"Isn't life wonderful post-Joel?" Zoe had her hair gelled into spikes and had rather overdone it with the eyeliner.

Camilla came racing up in a skirt the size of a hanky with a boy on each arm. She took one look at me and blanched in horror. "Oh my God. You've turned her into a teenage granny."

Zoe insisted the drudge look was the perfect way to win back Ash and I vowed at that moment to stand in dim lighting. "It's a known fact that boys like the innocent prim look," Zoe tried to convince me.

"There's prim and there's backward," Cam snorted in disgust. "What have you given her to read, *Pensioners Today*?

"Look, stop it both of you," I snapped. "I can sort out my own love life and my wardrobe." I stalked off towards the main door and realized the elastic was sagging in Zoe's brown skirt. It was roughly at that moment that Ruth glided past in a black sequinned number and I vowed that as soon as I'd received my trophy I was legging it as fast as I could.

The music was turned up full blast and the barn was chock-a-block with gyrating bodies.

"Hey Alex, good to see you. Cracking round." Damian Bevan hurtled past collecting empty Coke cans and looking as vacuous as ever.

Eric was over by the food table talking to Mrs Brayfield and trying to hide his boredom. Daisy was making a full recovery but he'd left her with Ash's parents for the night. I suddenly noticed the boy I'd been sitting next to at the slide show waving frantically and pushing his way towards me. Zoe grabbed my arm and we disappeared into a rugby scrum which turned out to be Camilla's cronies.

The loudspeaker crackled into life an hour later and then flipped off with a blown fuse. The music started up again with one of my favourite records and I honestly thought if the pain in my heart got any worse I'd have to sit down. Then I saw Ash, in his faded lemon shirt which showed off his suntan, dancing with Ruth who was as predatory as a panther.

"You've got to admit, she's got jungle cunning." Cam had detached herself from her admirers and was pouring me a drink.

"If I was in the jungle I'd only survive a few minutes," I whimpered, accepting the plastic cup.

"You'd need to grab hold of a lion's tail and let him pull you through." Cam gave me one of her sweetest smiles. "Some women need protecting, Alex, and you're one of them."

The music grew louder and I stood over in a corner listening to a group of boys eyeing up the talent. They were being spiteful about a girl I barely knew with fat legs. "It's a good job there's no lumberjacks in," one of them cackled. "They'd be felling her all night."

"Oh grow up," I snapped, letting my drink accidentally spill over his clean shirt. "You're pathetic."

Then I heard someone shout.

"Don't ever come near me again, I hate you!"

I knew that tinkly, over-sugared voice anywhere. I whipped round to see Ruth Hanson storm off the dancefloor in a flood of tears.

There was a chorus of wolf whistles and jibes and Ash stood rooted to the spot flushing every colour of the rainbow.

He didn't go after her.

"So the big romance has finally hit the rocks." Cam sidled up savouring the gossip. The whole room had hushed ten decibels; you could cut the atmosphere with a knife.

"Should somebody go after her?" Zoe looked concerned.

106

"Would you go after a tarantula?" Cam raised her perfectly plucked eyebrows. "I don't think so."

I was just about to insist on going across to Ash when the microphone coughed into life and the presentation got underway.

There weren't many prizes – one for the best turned out, one for the most improved rider, another for best beginner, etc, etc. I had to wait until the end for the challenge trophy.

Everyone clapped mechanically in the right places and yawned in the wrong places. Mrs Brayfield got the rosettes mixed up and one of the newest members twice misheard his name and went up for somebody else's prize.

Ash continually tried to catch my eye until I didn't know where to look.

"A huge round of applause everybody for our very own *chef d'équipe*, Eric Burgess." Mrs Brayfield held out a plain blue box and a matching rosette.

Eric cringed with embarrassment but put on a wooden smile and pushed his wheelchair forward. Suddenly there was a colossal clatter of cans and party poppers and Damian Bevan and co. shrieked into peals of laughter.

Eric took it in good spirit and Jasper immediately struck up with For He's a Jolly Good Fellow.

"Speech, speech." Everybody was shouting at once.

"Ladies and gentlemen, boys and girls." Eric nodded towards some of the younger members.

Mrs Brayfield passed over the blue box which was a small travel clock wrapped in tissue. It was lovely to see Eric so confident. "I'm proud to be involved with the Sutton Vale and here's to a long and happy future. Thank you."

"And good riddance to Joel!" Jasper yelled out, earning a severe scowl from Mrs Brayfield.

"Would Alexandra Johnson please come forward."

Toukie, who had won Most Improved Rider, was helping with the prizes.

"Good fancy dress outfit," someone shouted as I clung to the distressed elastic and decided from now on I would just be myself.

The challenge trophy was huge and Toukie was having great difficulty, only just realizing that the base was separate from the cup.

"Well done." Mrs Brayfield kissed my cheek and nearly tripped over some wires. Someone chucked a wilted flower forward and I almost imagined myself a famous ice skater.

Ash was clapping louder than anyone and his eyes flooded with warmth.

"Um, I'm not very good at this." I didn't know where to put my hands. "It's one thing to be receiving this trophy but I wouldn't be here if it wasn't for the team behind me. I've got a fantastic horse and a fantastic trainer. And I think, all in all, I must be the luckiest girl in the world."

"Hear, hear!" Someone bellowed from the back and I took a deep breath quick to stop my eyes filling up. Eric gave me an encouraging wink and then the lights dimmed and the music struck up.

It had been one of the most traumatic weeks of my life but we'd come through it with flying colours – "peak performance" Eric had called it and I'd never felt more proud in my life.

As everyone moved off to the dancefloor I sneaked out of the side door into the warm night air. I needed to be alone, just for a few minutes, to gather my thoughts. And there was someone special I wanted to see.

Barney was standing dozing by the field gate, his muscles rippling in the moonlight, his bottom lip falling open as he gently snored and snuffled asleep. Barney was the only horse I knew who could wake a whole stable yard with his snoring and the only horse who could catnap any time anywhere.

He jerked open one eyelid as I approached, carrying my shoes and wincing as the gravel stabbed my bare feet.

"Hello, sweetheart. Look what I've got to show you." I plonked the trophy down on the grass and stood back to admire it. Barney snorted with disdain and tried to raid my non-existent pockets. "From now on, darling," I gushed, "I'll never be taken in by anyone, I'll never push you too hard, never, you're so precious. I love you so much."

"They say talking to yourself is the first sign of madness." Ash sauntered out from behind a clump of trees, grinning his head off and carrying a paper plate. "Here, don't say I never give you dinner." He passed me the plate loaded up with party sausages and vol-au-vents.

"Uh, what's the matter? You couldn't find Ruth so you decided to make do with me?" The words escaped before I could stop them.

The pain shot across Ash's face. "You know, you ought to be renamed the Poisoned Dwarf. It's a peace offering – or don't you believe in compassion and forgiveness?"

"Forgiveness? That's rich – you go off with the first stupid airhead girl you meet and then expect to pick up where you left off."

"Well you did slag me off to everybody in the yard – all this rubbish about me being a useless kisser, and what about you fancying Jasper? I'd have thought you'd have more taste."

"W-what? Are you off your head?"

"Well, Ruth said that you—"

"Ruth seems to have been saying a lot of things . . . I presume you're not going to Paris?"

"Paris? Alex, what are you talking about?"

Barney suddenly butted me in the back so hard I went colliding into Ash's arms.

"Talk about being thrown together," I gasped, feeling his arms wind round me. "Do you think Barney's trying to tell us something?"

"That we've been stupid, pigheaded, and we're utterly made for each other?"

"That we've both been fools to listen to Ruth?"

"Oh Alex, you drive me mad, but you're so adorable. I've missed you so much."

"It's understandable." I burst into a fit of giggles when I saw the earnestness in his eyes. "You know, Mr Burgess, I really do think you mean it."

"Oh I do, I do." He bent his head to kiss me but I leant back just to prolong the moment.

"So you honestly never fancied Ruth?"

"Never – the girl's like a barnacle." He started waltzing me round and accidentally stood back in the plate of vol-au-vents. "Blondes may be my weakness, but Ruth was a peroxide – it doesn't count." He tickled me under the chin, his eyes dancing with mischief. "And I've fallen in love with a true blonde with a wild temper."

"And Sunshine Girl?"

"There'll be other horses – I think my career will survive. I was an idiot to try and string Ruth along until she signed me up. Will you ever forgive me?"

Suddenly Barney let out a piercing neigh and thumped the gate with a hind leg.

"I think he's trying to tell you to submit to my charms," Ash grinned.

My heart was soaring and my knees turned to jelly. It was a perfect moonlit summer evening and I had my two boys to share it with. As Ash kissed me I really didn't think I could be happier.

GLOSSARY

anti-cast roller   A stable **roller** which prevents the horse from becoming **cast** in the stable or box.

Badminton   One of the world's greatest three-day events, staged each year at Badminton House, Gloucestershire.

to **bank**   When a horse lands on the middle part of an obstacle (e.g. a **table**), it is said to have banked it.

bit   The part of the bridle which fits in the mouth of the horse, and to which the reins are attached.

bounce   A type of jump consisting of two fences spaced so that as the horse lands from the first, it takes off for the next, with no strides in between.

bridle   The leather **tack** attached to the horse's head which helps the rider to control the horse.

bullfinch   A flimsy hedge which the horse jumps/brushes through.

cast   When a horse is lying down against a wall

in a stable or box and is unable to get up, it is said to be cast.

chef d'équipe The person who manages and sometimes captains a team at events.

colic A sickness of the digestive system. Very dangerous for horses because they cannot be sick.

collected canter A slow pace with good energy.

cow hocks When the points of the horse's hocks are turned in, causing the toes to stick out and the horse to take short, rolling steps.

crop A whip.

cross-country A gallop over rough ground, jumping solid natural fences. One of the three eventing disciplines. (The others are **dressage** and **showjumping**.)

dressage A discipline in which rider and horse perform a series of movements to show how balanced, controlled, etc. they are.

dun Horse colour, generally yellow dun. (Also blue dun.)

ewe neck When the horse's neck is concave instead of being nicely arched.

feed room Store room for horse food.

forearm   The part of the foreleg between elbow and knee.

girth   The band which goes under the stomach of a horse to hold the **saddle** in place.

Grackle   A type of noseband which stops the horse opening its mouth wide or crossing its jaw. Barney is wearing one on the cover of *Will to Win*.

hand   A hand is 10 cm (4 in) – approximately the width of a man's hand. A horse's height is given in hands.

hard mouth   A horse is said to have a hard mouth if it does not respond to the rider's commands through the **reins** and **bit**. It is caused by over-use of the reins and bit: the horse has got used to the pressure and thus ignores it.

head collar   A headpiece without a **bit**, used for leading and tying-up.

hog's back   A jump which has a pole on either side and a top pole so that it has a rounded effect.

horsebox   A vehicle designed specifically for the transport of horses.

horse trailer   A trailer holding one to three horses, designed to be towed by a separate vehicle.

jockey skull   A type of riding hat, covered in brightly coloured silks or nylon.

jodhpurs   Type of trousers/leggings worn when riding.

lead rope   Used for leading a horse. (Also known as a "shank".)

livery   Stables where horses are kept at the owners' expense.

loose box   A stable or area, where horses can be kept.

manege   Enclosure for schooling a horse.

manger   Container holding food, often fixed to a stable wall.

martingale   Used to regulate a horse's head carriage.

numnah   Fabric pad shaped like a saddle and worn underneath one.

one-day event   Equestrian competition completed over one day, featuring **dressage**, **showjumping** and **cross-country**.

one-paced   Describes a horse which prefers to move at a certain pace, and is unwilling to speed up or increase its stride.

Palomino A horse with a gold-coloured body and white mane or tail.

Pelham bit A bit with a curb chain and two **reins,** for use on horses that are hard to stop.

Pony Club International youth organization, founded to encourage young people to ride.

reins Straps used by the rider to make contact with a horse's mouth and control it.

roach back When the horse's back sticks up instead of having a natural dip. Indicates a weak back.

roller Leather or webbing used to keep a rug or blanket in place. Like a belt or girth which goes over the withers and under the stomach.

saddle Item of tack which the rider sits on. Gives security and comfort and assists in controlling the horse.

showjumping A course of coloured jumps that can be knocked down. Shows how careful and controlled horse and rider are.

snaffle bit The simplest type of **bit**.

spread Type of jump involving two uprights at increasing heights.

square halt   Position where the horse stands still with each leg level, forming a rectangle.

steeplechasing   A horse race with a set number of obstacles including a water jump. Originally a cross-country race from steeple to steeple.

stirrups   Shaped metal pieces which hang from the saddle by leather straps and into which riders place their feet.

surcingle   A belt or strap used to keep a day or night rug in position. Similar to a **roller,** but without padding.

table   A type of jump built literally like a table, with a flat top surface.

tack   Horse-related items.

tack room   Where **tack** is stored.

take-off   The point when a horse lifts its forelegs and springs up to jump.

three-day event   A combined training competition, held over three consecutive days. Includes **dressage, cross-country** and **showjumping.** Sometimes includes roads and tracks.

tiger trap   A solid fence meeting in a point with a

large ditch underneath. Large ones are called elephant traps.

upright   A normal single showjumping fence.

Weymouth bit   Like a **Pelham bit,** but more severe.

A selected list of titles available from Macmillan and Pan Books

The prices shown below are correct at the time of going to press. However, Macmillan Publishers reserve the right to show new retail prices on covers which may differ from those previously advertised.

RIDERS

1. Will to Win	Samantha Alexander	£2.99
2. Team Spirit	Samantha Alexander	£2.99
3. Peak Performance	Samantha Alexander	£2.99
4. Rising Star	Samantha Alexander	£2.99
5. In the Frame	Samantha Alexander	£2.99
6. Against the Clock	Samantha Alexander	£2.99
7. Perfect Timing	Samantha Alexander	£2.99
8. Winning Streak	Samantha Alexander	£2.99

HOLLYWELL STABLES

1. Flying Start	Samantha Alexander	£2.99
2. The Gamble	Samantha Alexander	£2.99
3. Revenge	Samantha Alexander	£2.99
4. Fame	Samantha Alexander	£2.99

All Macmillan titles can be ordered at your local bookshop or are available by post from:

Book Service by Post
PO Box 29, Douglas, Isle of Man IM99 1BQ

Credit cards accepted. For details:
Telephone: 01624 675137
Fax: 01624 670923
E-mail: bookshop@enterprise.net

Free postage and packing in the UK.
Overseas customers: add £1 per book (paperback)
and £3 per book (hardback).